Space Traipse:

Hold My Beer

Season Two

Karina L. Fabian

I0617715

Laser Cow Press

Merritt Island, FL

Karina Fabian
Rockledge, FL
www.fabianspace.com

Book Layout ©2017 BookDesignTemplates.com
Cover art by Dawn Witzke

Space Traipse: Hold My Beer, Season 2/ Karina Fabian.—1st ed.
ISBN 978-1-7334471-1-9

To my husband. Here's to many years of binge-watching our favorite sci-fi and sharing a love of puns. You are the best man ever, an inspiration, and more fun than a trip to Rest Stop. I love you!

Space: By Keptar, there's a lot of it. And it's chock-full of stuff to do and people to meet. These are the adventures of the HMB Impulsive. Its mission: to explore worlds, to seek out anomalies, and to boldly do what no one else has the guts to do! And you know that we're the ship to do it.

Don't believe me? Hold my beer!

Contents

A Note on Vocabulary: Words evolve, especially when influenced by other cultures. This is true in the Space Traipse universe, too. In addition to some new alien words, there are some words – English and foreign – that are misspelled. This is deliberate in the case of slang and unique words. I also decided not to italicize them, since they are part of the ST:HMB vernacular. Italics are for emphasis.

Lone Star

Captains Log, Intergalactic Date 676889.4

The Impulsive is en route to Hydra Epsilon Six, a terrible name for a planet, but I'm sure we'll come up with something better soon. A Union deep space traffic hazard probe investigating an anomaly near there has sent back some unusual readings. If Union Central is correct, we may have found the generation ship, The Lone Star, which was lost three hundred years ago. We are to investigate and, if possible, make contact with or recover the craft and crew. I haven't been this excited about a mission in a long time, as it represents a bit of family history for me, as well.

Jebediah Tiberius, Captain of the HMB Impulsive and a Texan through and through, leaned forward in his seat as he watched the stars race by. It wasn't really the stars so much as a computer simulation of the scene in front of them. The real view was more a hyperactive rainbow kaleidoscope of space dust and radiation impacting on the deflector shields as the ship sped through space at a pace that would make a sane man blanch if he thought about it. And while "sanity" was a questionable attribute for most members of HuFleet, they nonetheless found the simulations more useful. So, white stars streaking by in a black field, occasionally interrupted by a cloudlike nebula, beautifully if inaccurately colored to show different gas types and to make good future screen savers.

"Are we there yet?" Jeb asked.

His helmsman, Lieutenant Tonio Cruz, spun in his seat, which was fine since they were on autopilot at this point. "You did not just ask me that again. *Mama mia!*" He returned his attention to his console, muttering in Italian about how they'd get there when they got there.

From the security console, Lieutenant Enigo LaFuentes said, "Maybe you shouldn't be too eager, Captain. If this genship is anything like The Hood, you could be in for some serious disappointment—if it even survived."

Around them, others nodded sagely. The Hood was a sister ship to the Lone Star, one of twenty generation ships sent to potentially habitable planets early in the human history of interstellar space travel. Of the ships, only two found habitable and uninhabited planets for colonization. Seven, including Lone Star, simply disappeared. Five met disastrous ends in the dangers of space, and two were captured by hostile aliens. One lost all its crew to disease; another to starvation when its food supply systems gave out. One, however, happened upon a Union ship, resulting in Earth joining its ranks.

The Hood, however, fell to gang wars that continue even today. The ship roams from planet to planet, stopping only long enough to pick up supplies and weapons before continuing on its way as its 600—1000 inhabitants (depending on the year and severity of the feuds) battle for control of the ship and its destiny. Now and again, someone in the Union thinks they should do something to separate the warring gangs, but at this point, no one wants them, and giving each their own genship would be akin to arming each with planet-killing weapons. Besides, sometimes something good comes out of the Hood, like the InstaStitcher, which can bind even a gut wound in three minutes or less.

And, of course, it produced Lt. LaFuentes, one of the most capable security officers in HuFleet. In the three days it'd taken to get to Hydra Epsilon Six, he'd run his security teams through several simulations and worst-case scenarios, basing them on his youthful memories of The Hood. The InstaStitcher had overheated four times already.

"I'll keep it in mind, Lieutenant, but I don't think that'll be the case. You gotta remember that this ship was funded, built, and manned by Texans. We're a pretty solid, unified lot. Besides, there were a lot of Seips on that ship; be good to know what happened to them."

"Seips?" LaFuentes asked.

"Yep. Kin on my momma's side. The Spacefaring Seips. They put their oil money into the space industry in the early Earth 2050s. Shoot, they owned most of the Lone Star. They were a keen and ruthless lot; they wouldn't have let civil war ruin their investment—or a pesky space anomaly, for that matter. Still, even if all we find is a husk, it clears up a missing branch of my family tree—no offense, Loreli."

Loreli, the xenologist and ship's sexy, smiled. "Of course not. I always thought the idiom amusing and complimentary, along with all the meanings of the human word, 'roots.'"

"Well, I'm glad you were able to pull up your roots and join us on the bridge once more. We missed you," the captain told the beautiful, plant-based woman, and the crew (particularly the men) heartily agreed. In addition to her regular duties, the ship's sexy was to remain unbelievably attractive and unattainable. She inspired the men and provided a welcome respite for wandering eyes, allowing the other women on the crew to get on with their jobs.

Alas, the men had no equivalent of a ship's sexy. They all had to stay trim and buff and attractive; fortunately, most women didn't need eye candy to work at top efficiency.

Loreli treated everyone to her signature smile, the one that made men's chests puff out just a bit. She'd gotten top marks for it in sexy training and practiced it regularly. Her body was really the result of good pruning; the human expressions, however, needed consistent exercise lest they become (pardon the expression) wooden.

While this amusing aside (that was mostly to introduce some of the main characters of the episode) happened, the Impulsive reached its destination. Cruz stopped the ship in front of what the screens showed to be a kind of wormhole, although the usual gravitational forces were not at work. The screen, therefore, showed only a slightly transparent darker spot in space rather than a matter-sucking void. From Ops, Ensign Ellie Doall explained this, adding that the odd readings the probe picked up both led into the void and emanated from it.

"The Lone Star's sensors were not as sophisticated as ours," she said. "They may not have seen it and crossed through. I'm getting some faint readings now… Sir, I think the ship is still there and functioning!"

Jeb twisted in his seat, grabbing the arm of his chair with one hand. With the other, he grabbed his butt, according to his new religion, Keptarianism. "By Keptar's cheek! They're alive?"

Doall frowned, and not just because her Captain was massaging his hiney. "I can't pick up life signs from here. I think I may be picking up transmissions, but I can't tell if they are human or intelligent in origin or just some automatic signal. Plus, there're some weird radiation bursts... Captain, I think it's weapons fire!"

"Weapon fire? Oh, hell, no! No one shoots at my kin just when I've found them. Cruz, can you take us through that hole?"

"It's not much bigger than the ship," Cruz complained. "It'll be like threading a needle. But fortunately, my nona was half-blind. I'm-a good at needles."

"Remind me to thank your nona. Smythe, put the ship on Yellow Alert until we're near the fighting, then switch us to red. LaFuentes, weapons hot, wait for my command, but then have at it. Doall—"

"I have the common frequencies used by Earth genships, and I'll start broadcasting as soon as we're in range," she concluded.

"Just tell me when we are. The first 'hello,' ought to be family. Ready, Cruz? Beer me."

Over the ship's comms, Smythe called for Yellow Alert. With ease of hundreds of drills and way-too-many real-life incidents, the crew sprang into action. The Impulsive's wikadas shields went up, angled close to the form of the ship and strongest where it might brush against the edge of the anomaly. Shift crewmen on breaks secured whatever they were doing and hurried back to stations, while those already there prepared for battle or other turbulence by securing loose objects and taking the future's equivalent of Dramamine if they were faint of stomach. Second shift prepared themselves, in case they needed to replace a fallen comrade, while third shift mostly put on sleep masks and engaged secure covers mode. Somebody had to be well-rested to clean up the aftermath or come to the rescue.

Once all sections reported ready, Cruz guided the Impulsive through the anomaly. In a TV show, there would be a three-minute stretch of long-view scenes interspersed with close-ups of worried crew members, but we all know Cruz got them through. However, if you want mood music and are reading the ebook and have the tech savvy, I suggest pulling up Feral Chase by Kevin McLoed. Listen and rub your face, Kirk style. If you have a print copy, use your imagination.

...

Okay? Ready to move on?

"Didn't even scratch the paint," Cruz said proudly as they passed through. He engaged the hyperdrive to maximum. After a few empty minutes of people triple-checking their stations and wondering if they were going to see action or if they gave up their shot at the high score of Broxie for nothing, they entered the system.

The Lone Star was a Class C Deep Space Generation Colonization ship. A mile and a half long in the center, with the bridge on one end, thrusters on the other and engineering through the core, its thick corridor spokes spanned out half a mile out to link it to the dual habitation circles. Each a mile in diameter at the outside, the circles rotated at 212 feet/second, generating a full Earth G of gravity. Take away the solar panels and it looked like a weird kids' science toy that seemed cool on the commercials but only kept your child's interest for all of ten minutes before being tossed aside for yet another first-person shooter game, or in the case of toddlers, the toilet plunger.

More importantly, the ship was indeed firing upon the surface, and someone on the planet was firing back. Doall reported that the settlement under attack looked industrial in purpose, but heavily fortified and protected by shields similar to the ones protecting the Lone Star. There were similar shield bubbles around other small areas fanning out from the settlement. Outside the shields, she detected life signs—human and humanoid.

Smythe called for Red Alert, and LaFuentes reported weapons ready and shields up.

"If those are the best weapons they got, we're not in any danger," LaFuentes announced. "Want me to prep a peacekeeping team to teleport over?"

"Thank you, Lieutenant, but let's get our facts straight before we send anyone."

Doall announced they were in communications range and were being warned off by both sides.

Jeb straightened in his seat and put on his thickest, friendliest accent. "Ensign, open a channel to both sides—visuals, if they can receive them. Lone Star, unidentified colony, this is Captain Jebediah Seip Tiberius of the HMB Impulsive. We don't mean to pry, but we'd sure like to visit, and if we can help..."

The Impulsive's screen opened a second window (computer, not literal, which would be idiotically fatal), and a man in a blue uniform with archaic military rank on it appeared. The background showed him to be in command of the Lone Star. "What trickery is this? You sure as hell don't look Paleo. How did they contact you?"

A woman who had been seated pensively in the back suddenly leaped up and shoved the man out of the way. "Billy, don't be rude. Are you really a Seip-Tiberius? The Tiberiuses were ranchers."

"Still are, ma'am. You're talking to a genuine space cowboy. Who might this be?"

The woman laughed. "Well, you have the Seip humor and humility, to be sure. So you're really from Earth? Oh, bless your timing! This is Donna Bel, former First Officer of the Lone Star, now retired. Please help us—help me! That's our colony down there we're shooting the snot out of, and they've already damaged several of our systems..."

"Aunt DeeBee!" Billy interjected, but she continued, anyway.

"The captain—my Bobby—is down there, supposedly to discuss a truce with his brother, J.R., but now they're fighting and no one is listening to reason. People are taking sides. The habitat levels are on lockdown... It's all-out war. Why is that man behind you rolling his eyes?"

Everyone on the bridge turned to look at their Chief of Security, who chose the better part of valor and focused on his console. He bit down on his mouth to avoid saying, "Told you so."

* * *

Captain's Log, Intergalactic Date 676889.55

The excitement of finding the Lone Star after it had been lost for centuries has been overshadowed by tragedy. The command staff of the ship are at war with the colony that they started on the surface of the planet they've named "Alamo." Apparently, the issues are convoluted, so much so even the Lone Star's bridge crew got to arguing when they tried to explain it.

I have decided to heed Lieutenant LaFuentes' suggestion and establish peacekeeping operations. The Impulsive now stands between the warring factions. Our shields can take the beating, no problem. We're taking a small security force to the surface to retrieve the two brothers and see if we can't talk some sense into them.

Lt. LaFuentes had recommended that they teleport to a hill a couple of hundred yards away from the fighting and that his minions be armed with CrowdStunner 3000s. Jeb had doubts when he saw the gleeful looks on the faces of some of the security team, but LaFuentes was the expert in this situation, both by training and personal experience. Besides, he had shown restraint in not saying "I told you so" on the bridge, so Jeb was willing to cut him some slack.

They had taken position on the teleport pad in a circle, facing outward, with Jeb and LaFuentes in the center. They all crouched to make as low a target as possible.

"Ready, Chief?" Jeb asked the teleporter chief, Dolfrick Dour.

"You shall all die by my hand and thus be remade," he intoned.

"Just the way we like it! Beer us."

They materialized as expected on the hill, unnoticed by the fighting crowd. Although a civil war, it resembled more of a tavern brawl, thanks to all the hand-to-hand fighting. Men and women dressed similarly in blue jeans and work shirts swung, kicked, and charged each other. Interspersed among them were other, alien humanoids, distinguishable because they were shorter and stockier, with longer arms. Most bore colorful tattoos, visible where sleeves ended or clothes were torn. There was no shortage of torn shirts and quite a bit of blood, but most of the bodies on the ground were cussing and moaning.

"You know," Jeb said as he scanned the field with binoculars for the men matching D.B.'s description, "I don't think anyone wants to do permanent harm."

"For now, anyway," LaFuentes said. He scanned the field with his own binoculars, then pointed to where two men were fighting near a rock outcropping. "There's our targets. Wide range stun. Cut us a swath and spread out from there."

"Are you sure that's necessary?"

"Headaches save lives!" The security officers, jazzed at actually getting to put their training to use, began firing with controlled abandon. The CrowdStunner 3000s shot out wide beams, filling the air with cones of pale yellow, which actually had nothing to do with the energy itself, but had been added by the manufacturers so people knew where the beam ended and could jump out of the way. They said it was for safety, but most people thought it gave the other side a sporting chance. In this case, however, the technology was so advanced compared to that of the Lone Star's that the inhabitants didn't make the connection, even if they had turned their attention away from decking each other to notice.

Once the closest combatants were taking dirt naps, the team moved forward, keeping the protective circle. Those in the back and looking behind pouted internally about not having more targets. Soon the fighters noticed what was going on. The natives—and a couple of less intelligent humans—charged the team and were put to sleep for their bravado. Others tried to draw weapons. LaFuentes and Jeb took them out with hand rasers also on stun. After that, a few ran, but most tried to get a slug or two in before retreating. They got stunned, too.

Bobby and J.R. heard the commotion—or mostly the choruses of "Uhnn!"-plop!—and stopped to face the Impulsive team. J.R. called for retreat and ran, but Bobby pulled out a gun.

Jeb held up his hands. "Don't shoot!"

LaFuentes dropped the Lone Star captain.

Jeb sighed. "Well, that's going to make talking to him that much harder." He paused to look around, saw that everyone was an Impulsive crewman or passed-out, and broke through the circle of security to approach the unconscious captain. He nudged him with his foot and rolled him over. The man snored.

"I had it on the lightest setting—30 minutes or thereabouts," LaFuentes said. "The rest will be out for an hour."

"All right, then. Bring down some more security and some medical staff, and let's see what we can mend. In the meantime, I'll take Bobby here to the Impulsive. If his brother comes back, try to get him to join us, without shooting him if possible."

He tapped his comm badge and called for teleport. As the sparkle took over him and his lost kinsman, a woman ran out from behind the rocks and threw herself into his arms.

* * *

This wasn't the first time Teleporter Chief Dour had teleported an embracing couple onto a ship, but this was the first time he'd teleported the captain in the arms of a stranger. One of the Lone Star crew, then—pre-teleport technology. He sighed. Another victim sacrificed to his goddess. And there was another one, crumpled at their feet. Did he want to know?

Not really. The point was, they had both been pure once. Now, his mistress had soiled them with her arcane technological touch. He sent a command to his personal replicator for clean robes and test tubes, then recorded their data on microwires.

Meanwhile, the female had disengaged herself and was looking around with wonder. She was a buxom woman, dressed in tight pants that flared at the ankles to make room for her boots.

Her hair was brunette, wavy and messy enough to indicate some exertion. She had tanned skin and large, blue eyes. She reminded him of the girls his sister hung around with, always reprogramming their hair and makeup bots and trying to outdo each other for Miss Congeniality.

She turned back to the captain, the curiosity in her expression making her seem younger. "Where are we? How did we get here?"

"Well, Ma'am, you hitched a ride."

"And destroyed yourself in the process," Dour concluded. Then, seeing her pale in shock, added, "You got better. Captain, shall I call a medical team for the other one?"

"Yes, thank you. He's just stunned. Some caffeine and an analgesic, and he'll be fine, but let's get him to Sickbay, so he knows we care. In the meantime, ma'am, I'm Captain Jebediah Seip-Tiberius. And you are…"

The woman was examining the teleporter ceiling as if longing to know its secrets. "Sue Ellen. Sue Ellen Loggins Seip. J.R.'s my husband. You're the ones who tried to contact us, aren't you? I tried to get them to listen, but J.R.'s second is as stubborn as an aft thruster. I ran to find J.R., and there you were, just striding through the battle, your men cutting down the opposition like a lawnmower before game day."

Jeb grimaced. "They can get a little enthusiastic."

"They were magnificent! And my husband just up and ran, so I knew someone had to take his place. I didn't think. I just ran to you. I, I hope I wasn't too forward."

From the console, Dour watched how she sidled a little closer and looked up at the captain coyly. Dour kept his opinions to himself. He really wanted them to leave so he could start his cleansing ritual.

The doors opened, and a medical team with a gurney stepped through. As they loaded the sleeping man, the captain offered the woman his arm and told her he thought she could be of great help to them, but as they had a few minutes, they could take the long route and see some of the ship.

Just as they exited, a delivery bot zipped through the closing doors, bearing Dour's robes, scanner, and tools. He nodded to himself. The teleporter was the only mistress he desired.

* * *

Captain Tiberius often led tours of the ship. Seldom, however, did he have his visitor cling so tightly to him while trying to look around. He couldn't say he minded, though he wished the woman in question was not an in-law, no matter how far removed. It made thoughts of romance uncomfortable.

Most crewmen greeted them with studious ignorance, as if some kind of HuFleet training kept them from seeing how she arched her back so her bosom pressed against his arm. If he'd had that training, he could use a refresher, he decided. It was a relief when Minion Torez from Engineering greeted him by slapping his own butt.

"Kra Keptar, Captain!"

"Fruliogri Kra, Torez," he replied and slapped his own derriere. As they passed each other, they reached out to squeeze the other's cheek. It was the right, not the left, but Sue Ellen was clinging to his left side. He was sure Keptar would understand.

"My goodness! What in the universe was that about?" she asked.

"Standard Keptarian blessing," Jeb explained. "I and some of the crew converted to the religion after rescuing an alien vessel. Keptar is the great force that spewed out the gasses of the universe that coalesced to become the stars and planets we roam today. Even we are the result of his great expulsion."

"Fascinating! And the, well, butt-smacking?"

He grinned. He did so love this part. "Well, the exact theology is complex. I'm still learning the intricacies. Think of it as part blessing, part witness, part call to action."

He stopped in front of a viewport, and with a stunning display of an extrapolated panorama of the stars opposite the planet as a backdrop, he disengaged himself from her grasp to demonstrate. He smacked his own behind. "Keptar's buttocks are the seat of life, get it? So we are called to keep our own seats firm, yet supple, as a reminder to keep our hearts and minds the same. As our behinds go, so shall our lives. So, when Keptarians greet each other, we slap to show resolve and grab to support and to remind the other to stay worthy."

Sue Ellen gave a small gasp. "That is so deep! But aren't all worthy?"

"On this ship? No doubt. But everyone has the potential, even if it's not fulfilled. Prayers are a workout, I can assure you."

She giggled, then rubbed her own posterior thoughtfully. "Do you think...I'd be worthy?"

In the name of Keptar, he took hold of her left buttock in the ritual five-finger spread for evaluating a potential acolyte. He smiled reassuringly. "I don't think you have anything to worry about."

Then he offered her his arm and they started back along the corridor. "If you're really interested, when we're done with this mix-up, I'll give you some literature. But right now, why don't you tell me what got this whole feud started?"

She pouted. "What always sets brother against brother? Desire for power and general pig-headedness. Bobby can tell you the details—from his side, anyway. Jimmy Ray will have his own story. And the truth will be somewhere between, if there is a truth. I'm afraid I'm not much help to you. I wasn't involved, you see, with all the behind-the-scenes of the settlement."

"What did you do on the Lone Star?"

"Oh, I was Chief Hospitality Officer—you know, managing the activities and the upkeep and general morale-building? It's a difficult job, even more so when the power problems started, and then the fighting... There's only so much football and cotillions can do. I... Excuse me."

She stopped and let him go to wrap an arm around herself. The other, she used to press her fist against her mouth. Her eyes started to glisten with tears she blinked back.

Jeb's heart softened, and like a true Texan, he felt the urge to console her and beat some sense into the idjits who made this pretty filly cry. "Hey, now. It'll be all right. We'll talk some sense into both parties. In the meantime, we're close to the Impulsive's rec facility. Want to drop in and take a look?"

She wiped the single tear that escaped, then brightened. "I'd love to!"

* * *

The captain had left LaFuentes with a difficult situation. He had six men to keep over 200 combatants at bay. That, itself, was not the problem. Ordinarily, he'd set up two restraining fields and separate sides. However, here, there was no way to tell who was on which side. No one wore colors, and while a few wore ship uniforms, there weren't enough to indicate the army—plus a few uniformed people were fighting each other, so it probably wasn't a good indicator, anyway.

In the end, he took a lesson from his childhood. While his team and the medical team started separating people by injury, he had Security replicate and send down PunchBacks for each combatant, plus more of his minions.

The Lone Star crew and the natives awoke to find themselves in groups of 20 held in containment fields guarded by a security officer armed with a CrowdStunner. The groups were in a half circle focused on LaFuentes. Behind him was a holographic screen.

"All right! Listen up!" he said when a sufficient number of people had awakened and taken stock of their situation. His voice was amplified and projected through the communicators of his team, so everyone could hear him. Several folks winced at the sound, but they quieted. "I'm Lieutenant Enigo Guiermo Ricardo Montoya Guiterrez LaFuentes, Security Chief of the HuFleet ship, Impulsive. We got no argument with anyone here, understand? We got sent from HuFleet—Earth—to find you, and we're not going to go back and tell them we watched you blow each other up. At least, not until we tried to make peace. Now, my captain is trying to talk sense into your leaders—"

He was interrupted as several folks tried to strike their neighbor and promptly screamed in pain.

"Ai! I'm talking, here! Shuddap and listen. *Callate!* Now, look. My job is to keep you guys from beating each other to pulps while my captain talks sense into your leaders. Every one of you is wearing a device that measures the force and speed of your extremities. Try to punch, kick, or head-butt your neighbor and you get the zap of your life."

"That's it?" one burly guy said. "If I try to punch a good-fer-nothin' SOB next to me, I get shocked?"

LaFuentes knew what he was getting at. There always had to be one, but he did appreciate that someone asked questions. Showed they were paying attention. He made sure the camera projecting to the screen was focused on the man before he answered. "Yeah. Harder you try, the more it hurts you."

"Worth it!" He gritted his teeth and swung at the man next to him.

LaFuentes stunned him.

"He'll wake up in a few minutes," LaFuentes assured the crowd as the man crumpled live and on holo. "Hopefully, a little wiser for his curiosity. We can stun you all again if we have to. If you guys want to sort yourselves out, we can make accommodations. Otherwise, sit tight. Captain Seip-Tiberius will no doubt smooth things out between your leaders."

"And if he doesn't?" a young woman with a swelled lip asked.

LaFuentes shrugged. "We'll finish patching up the injured and teleport out of here, taking the restraints with us, and you can go back to your happy little war. Don't matter to me. I grew up on the Hood.

"In the meantime, if you're curious about what's been happening in the rest of the universe while you were gone, the ship's historian Lieutenant Ashton Leito is going to give you a crash course on the past three centuries."

He gave them a nod and went to check on the wounded. He figured someone else would try their luck eventually, but his people could handle it. Besides, Leito was a good lecturer; funny as well as informative.

"Good speech, sir," Minion II said as he approached. They stood together outside swinging range of any of the wounded and watched as the medical team used the InstaStitch on lacerations, the bone knitter on breaks, and imposazine on just about everything else. LaFuentes had suggested to the doctor that he leave the bruises and at least a scar or two so they could remember the incident. The doctor was also running a scanner over an unconscious native, getting readings.

II continued. "Great idea about the PunchBacks, too. Could I ask you something, though? Without you stunning me?"

He snorted. "You ask smart questions, Il. What is it?"

"Well, the PunchBacks. They were used on the Hood, right? Didn't it lead to one of the bloodiest rebellions in your history?"

"Sort of. They're alien tech, remember? And the effects were much worse. You could end up in a coma for bloodying some benndero's nose. The Dread Oogs of the Coe Nebula used them to enslave us while they tried to teach us empathy and social awareness. So yeah, we also had a two-year cease-fire among the gangs. Then, we worked around the tech and killed them all and half their fleet besides. Once our common enemy was gone, it was back to gang warfare."

He grinned at the memories. He'd been seven, aware enough of the animosity against the Crips, the Spanners, and the Spokeriders, but young enough to have enjoyed a pick-up game of basketball. (Rugby and Lacrosse, of course, had proven too painful for everyone.) Sometimes, he wondered if those years of peace had contributed to his wanting to join HuFleet. If so, he was glad for it, even if at nine, he'd scored his first kill by taking out a Dread Oog during the revolt. Good times.

He shrugged. "Anyway, don't worry about it. They won't be wearing them for long. The captain will get this figured out."

His communicator beeped—a message from the Impulsive. "Lieutenant, it's Gel. You've got company coming. Four humans and two alien. They aren't being especially stealthy, though. They may want to talk."

"Nova. Let the captain know, and ask if he wants them to come aboard. Tell him, I'll try to keep them conscious."

A burble of amusement told him Gel got the joke. "Aye, L.T. Gel out."

"LaFuentes out." He tapped off the communicator and called over two of his minions. It was time to meet the neighbors.

* * *

Jeb and Sue Ellen were chuckling together as they entered Sickbay. Her light laughter stopped when she saw her brother-in-law laying on the medbed, on his side, monitors above him clicking and displaying numbers she didn't understand.

"Bobby!" She rushed to his side.

"Don't worry. He's recovered, just sleeping."

In confirmation, Bobby let out a snore. The pillow had a damp spot.

"Wake him, please," the captain said.

The nurse nodded and grabbed the man's shoulder. "Sir? It's time to wake up, sir. Come on, wakey-wakey, no more breaky."

The man moaned and opened his eyes. "Ellie? Where...?"

Then he moaned in earnest as the raser-induced headache hit. The nurse handed him a pill. Without even a token of suspicion, he snagged it and swallowed it and the entire glass of water she gave him.

"We're on the Human Fleet ship Impulsive," Ellie said, her voice soft in deference to the pain in his head. "This is Captain Jebediah Seip-Tiberius. He's come to help us make peace."

Bobby's head had to be feeling better, but he scowled as if it pained him, nonetheless. "There can be no peace, Sue Ellen, until my brother puts aside his selfish ways. Has she explained, Captain?"

Jeb nodded. It hadn't been easy to get her to stop her flirting and asking him to demonstrate

Keptarian prayer exercises, but he'd gotten the highlights. "He's started a settlement to drill for liquid unobtanium, which the Lone Star needs in order to return back to Earth. But you assert that it's having a detrimental effect on the environment, including the natives."

"Detrimental?" Bobby shouted, then winced. "Captain, he'll kill the native population—and even worse, he's convinced them that it's a good thing!"

"The natives we saw seemed pretty hale."

"Oh, the Paleos are fine—for a while. We should never have started drilling. Part of me knew it, too. We were desperate, Captain, on our last reserves, no way back. We've been seeking a way home for almost three hundred years, and we finally found the anomaly that had brought us here, but we didn't have the fuel to push through. Then we found the unobtanium on this world. We thought we'd set up drilling in an uninhabited place.

"It turns out it was a sacred spot. We desecrated it, yet the people were so kind, forgiving. We told ourselves we'd just take enough to fuel the ship, then we'd be on our way.

Then, the changes started. Something about the drilling is releasing a chemical into the air. It's harmless to humans, but not the aliens. They breathe it in. They feel superior—but it's an illusion, Captain, a pleasant dream that they're sacrificing their lives and their culture for."

His expression hardened. "Now, J.R. won't leave. He thinks he can set himself up as some kind of god, drain this planet dry—resources and civilizations!"

"Bobby, that's not fair!" Sue Ellen interjected, but it was a weak protest.

"Isn't it? You've seen how the Paleos are changed. You know what comes next. Captain Tiberius, you have to help me stop my brother from committing genocide!"

* * *

Lieutenant LaFuentes and his two security minions took position at the top of the hill—which is to say, they were scattered in strategic positions and crouched behind rocks just in case the approaching contingent of Lone Star members and aliens decided to start shooting. They watched as the others strode toward them along the saddle between hills. A couple of drones had preceded the contingent and overflown the camp. Since the drones weren't armed, LaFuentes had let them pass.

When they got within shouting distance, LaFuentes called out. "That's far enough! Throw down your weapons and state your business."

"This is our planet!" a human with an accent to rival Captain Tiberius's hollered back. "Who the hell are you to tell us what to do?"

"We're the peacekeeping force from... Earth," LaFuentes shouted back. He'd actually never been to humankind's planet of origin, himself, but if these guys didn't know about the Union, it was safer to give them something familiar to identify with.

However, the speaker latched onto a different detail. "Peacekeeping? You've gone and imprisoned my people."

"The other side, too. Been pretty peaceful ever since. We're tending your wounded, too. You're welcome. I'm Lieutenant LaFuentes of the HMB Impulsive. Who are you?"

"I'm James Ray Seip, leader of Alamo. Beside me is Chi Nikki Chawa; he's the elected leader of the Evolved Paleos."

"That some kind of gang?" LaFuentes wished Loreli were there. She'd love this. He renewed his vows to bring some of them up conscious.

"No. I can explain everything, Lieutenant. My brother, Bobby, is trying to sabotage our only way home, and he's stopping the advancement of the indigenous peoples. I'm sure we can straighten all this out. Come down here and let's talk."

"We can hear each other just fine. But if you want to come closer, lay down your weapons and put your hands in the air."

Chi Nikki Chawa stepped toward them—but just one stride. Whether he was trying to upstage Seip or protect him, LaFuentes wasn't sure, but since he stopped at the single step, he held his fire.

Chi Nikki Chawa said in perfect English: "What kind of honorless coward are you, that you hide behind rocks and aim weapons at us while we talk peace?"

LaFuentes laughed, loud, and he thought he'd heard his team chuckle, too. They both knew better than to fall for that bait; they'd seen his scars. "Man, the first and last time I fell for that line I was fourteen. I got no reason to trust you."

"And what reason do we have to trust you?" Chawa retorted.

"We've held a couple hundred of your people captive for over two hours, and so far all we've done is keep them quiet, given them a catch-up history lesson, and fixed their injuries."

For a wonder, Chawa seemed satisfied with the answer. He tossed down the primitive spear he'd been holding and followed it up with his pistol. James watched, then shrugged and tossed down his guns as well. Only the two of them, however. The rest took out their weapons and trained them toward the Impulsive team.

LaFuentes found that sensible and respectable. "Gracias, man. Okay, listen. Our captain wants to talk to you, so I'm going to toss you down a device."

"A communicator?"

"Yeah, but it's also a location beacon. We're gonna teleport you to our ship. Your brother and some chica are already there."

"Sue Ellen?" J.R. asked.

"She didn't say her name. She just jumped in the captain's arms as he was teleporting to the ship."

"Sue Ellen," J.R. concluded, and he didn't sound too happy about it. LaFuentes sent a quiet warning to Gel to prepare for a potential domestic, then tossed down the extra communicator he'd brought. Chawa picked it up and looked it over curiously.

"Now what?" James demanded.

"Hold still. It may tickle. Dour, three to 'port up."

It wasn't often that Chief Dour teleported people for the first time, let alone five uninitiated in under a day. It gave him mixed feelings. While he mourned the loss of the original, with its virginal molecules unsullied by the machinations of his mistress, he nonetheless had a strong curiosity about people's reactions after their first time.

Sue Ellen had been fascinated and elated, which, given the fact that she'd arrived in the captain's embrace, seemed perfectly suited to her personality. Typical. The human who arrived looked surprised and a little shaken. Again, not an unusual reaction. Disappointing.

The alien, however… He gasped, drawing a huge draught of air, as though he'd felt smothered by the process. He staggered, wrapped his arms around himself protectively as if anticipating his body flying apart into a trillion subatomic particles. He scanned the room wildly, and when his eyes alighted on the teleporter console, they widened with existential dread. Dour could see the man's intellect fighting against the instinctive urge to throw himself before the console in supplication and fear.

Dour found this sensible and respectable.

"What have you done to us?" the alien whispered in his own language. The ship's translator repeated it, even to the same awed, horrified tone.

LaFuentes broke the moment. "Aw, take it easy. I promise, whatever you had on the planet you still got now, and it's all in the same place. Come on. I'll take you to the captain."

LaFuentes waved a hand toward the door. The human slapped his alien companion on the shoulder in a comradely way, and he regained his composure. LaFuentes escorted them out. As he passed by the console, he gave Dour's robes a once over and rolled his eyes.

When the doors closed behind them, Dour intoned, "And thus does another moment of death and resurrection befall a new species, only to be brushed aside with the banality of human concerns."

He needed to have another ritual. But first, he wanted to record this moment in poetry. It was deliciously depressing.

* * *

Captain's Log… Computer, stick a timestamp on there, 'kay? Thanks.

Let's see… So far, we've found my long-lost kin on the brink of a feud over how to treat the locals, and we've had to break up one fight and are keeping the parties separate until we can talk sense into them. Their ship is out of fuel and needs a tow home. Oh, and my gorgeous in-law is hitting on me. Damn, we just need a keg and a green-bean casserole, and it'd be like any other family reunion.

Lieutenant LaFuentes has brought up my cousin, Jimmy Ray, brother to Bobby Joe, the Captain of the Lone Star, and was sleeping off a raser stun in our sickbay. Meanwhile, Loreli has successfully charmed the First Officer of the Lone Star, who has told his troops on the planet to stand down. Most were glad enough to do so, as Lt. Leito is showing them a dramatization of our first contact with the Logics. Yeah, I remember that one from my first year at the Academy. I don't think I laughed so hard in class before or since.

In deference to Bobby's headache, Jeb led him and Sue Ellen to the nearest conference room and had the raser-struck captain comfortably ensconced in a chair. Loreli joined them as well. They had just finished introductions by the time Lt. LaFuentes arrived with J.R. and Chi Nikki Chawa in tow.

"J.R!" Ellie ran from her seat and threw her arms around her husband. He allowed but did not return her embrace, instead using the opportunity to scan the room with narrowed eyes. When his gaze alighted on Loreli, he looked her over with open appreciation. Enigo's fist curled, and he made a note to ensure the human never got a chance to be alone with their ship's sexy. From her side of the table, Loreli cataloged the expression on J.R.'s face, noting Enigo's clenched fist and making the same vow.

Sue Ellen leaned back. "J.R., honey?"

"You'll explain yourself later." He moved away from her, toward his brother. "You okay?"

"'Cept for the headache from their stun gun, yeah."

"That's not from the stun gun. That's from my fist."

"You wish!" he retorted, then the two broke into snickers. "Jimmy Ray, meet Captain Jebediah Seip-Tiberius, who happens to be a distant cousin."

"And that gives you the right to stick your nose in our business?" J.R. demanded.

Jeb held up his hands placatingly. "A lot has happened in the three centuries you've been lost...including some rules about when I can stick my nose into other people's business. One is to break up a fight. Another is to protect the indigenous species of a planet."

J.R. turned to Chi Nikki Chawa. "Why, Chi Nikki Chawa, do you need protecting from us—from me?"

"No. In fact, your actions have been foretold in our prophecy. I praise what you have done for us. I would not be the man I am today were it not for your people." He turned to sneer at Bobby.

Bobby frowned back. "Today, perhaps. But in fifteen, twenty years? What you will be, Chi Nikki Chawa, is dead, and you know it."

"Lies!" J.R. hollered.

"Fact! Since we started mining the unobtanium and exposed the local population, nearly a hundred of them have died—ten times the normal death rate!"

"And those who survived are stronger, smarter, and more capable. Captain Tiberius, not that it's any of your business, understand, but my brother here would have you think I'm some kind of greedy, capitalist murderer. We went down there to get fuel so we could go home—but I stayed down there and fought my own kind to give the Paleos a chance at a better civilization. You need proof? Send someone down to their villages. The people are primitive and stupid."

"Careful," Chi Nikki Chawa warned. "They are still my people and worthy of respect."

"Respect?" Bobby said, pressing his advantage. "Do you see at last? Jimmy Ray looks at your people and equates lack of technology with lack of intelligence."

Sue Ellen pleaded, "Now, boys, let's not fight in front of company."

J.R. ignored her. "Oh, please! You look at their hand-made tools and fur blankets and think they're noble, when they're just living in squalor. Meanwhile the Evolved Paleos—"

"Oh! So it's not a gang," LaFuentes burst out.

Bobby looked at him for the first time. "Hey! You're the one that shot me."

"I'll do it again if you don't calm down."

"All right. I think we all need to calm down," Jebediah said, including himself even though he was perfectly in control. It was one of those things diplomats did, he knew. The good ones could even make it sound like they weren't patronizing at all. Apparently, he got it right, because the brothers both took breaths and relaxed their postures, although they still threw each other angry looks.

"Now, see here," Jebediah continued, "we've got some pretty heavy accusations going on, and your momma gave our xenologist an earful, too. However, with the technology on the Impulsive, it should be pretty easy to determine if the unobtanium mining is indeed killing people, and maybe even find a way to stop that."

"They don't want to stop that—I mean the effects of the unobtanium. That's what I'm trying to tell you!"

Loreli nodded her head toward J.R., a simple motion that nonetheless brought every eye to her. She gave both Seip men and the Evolved Paleo her Understanding Smile No. 5, the one that nonverbally communicated that she thought they had vital points and she was totally on their side...even though the subjects of her smile were on opposite sides. "I think an interested but unemotionally-invested third party can perhaps shed some light on these concerns. I'm fascinated by the idea that prophecy plays a role in all this, and I'd like to compare the quality of life for both the Evolved and the...unchanged Paleos."

She stood. "Captain, with your permission, I'd like to go to the surface and observe."

J.R. suddenly puffed up his chest. "Well, then, missy. I'd be honored to escort you."

Still at his side, Sue Ellen gasped in outrage.

Enigo said, "Don't you think you'd do more good here with the captain—and your *wife*?"

J.R. spun on him. His face was flushed, his muscles tensed. "Who do you think you are, telling me what to do?"

Enigo didn't answer his question, but he stood ready to reply to his challenge.

Chi Nikki Chawa stepped between them. "They are my people. I am welcome among them. With permission, I shall escort Green Woman Loreli."

"I think that's a fine idea," Sue Ellen said frostily. She had also shifted position—between her husband and the beautiful Botanical.

Jeb bit back a smile. He loved it when other people solved their own problems without him interfering. "Well, that's settled. Lieutenant LaFuentes, why don't you escort Lieutenant Loreli—and pick up the doctor, too. He can probably run some scans on the natives and give us a better idea of what's going on, biologically speaking."

Chi Nikki Chawa gave the captain a small bow. "Thank you, Captain. I do not think my people would enjoy a trip through your teleporters."

"They wouldn't be the only species. LaFuentes, be sure to contact the doctor first and see if he needs any special equipment 'ported down. He wasn't expecting much more than minor medical procedures."

His officers took that as dismissal. Loreli moved around the table with practiced ease, but she toned down her usual sway and made sure to pass by the group still standing at the door so that Enigo was between her and J.R. LaFuentes, in turn, stuck close to her side, one hand protectively hovering over the small of her back. With the other, he directed Chi Nikki Chawa to precede them. Normally, men (and some women) opened doors for Loreli to go through first, but Enigo grew up knowing you always put potential threats in front of you where you could see them.

Of course, that also meant that the door opened to find two security guards on the other side, who glared past Chi Nikki Chawa, Loreli, and LaFuentes, to the frowning human male who had had been posturing against their superior officer. Enigo also knew you always had backup ready, just in case.

At Sickbay, one of the nurses prepared a backpack with scanning equipment. To be more precise, the backpack was the scanner, with a handheld device connected wirelessly to the main console. The portable device would allow the doctor or medical technician to run a complete set of scans for analysis.

Actually, anyone could run the scans. It's not hard to wave a flashy light tube over a person. However, most people felt weird about the average joe invading their personal bubble, except when that "joe" was in medical or security. Thus, in a feat of standardization that could only happen in a bright and most-likely impossible future, all scanner wands worked the same way, whatever data it recorded.

Every doctor and security officer in HuFleet had to take a three-week course in scanner wand waving. Enigo had then further honed his skills during a six-week stint at HuFleet HQ, scanning visitors for nanoexplosives and surveillance devices. While it had been a punishment for starting a bar fight, it nonetheless made him one of the most qualified people on the Impulsive to run the medical scanner.

It also meant he got to carry the backpack.

Loreli grinned as he grumbled about not being able to do his job protecting them if he had to protect equipment on his back. "When we get to the teleporter room, I'll don the pack."

Enigo grinned at her. "Then the doctor will have to do the chivalrous thing and take it from you. I didn't know you had such a conniving mind, Fronds."

Loreli had the computer explain chivalry to Chi Nikki Chawa as they made their way to the teleporter room. It didn't take long. Apparently, their people had a similar concept. "Though, it's usually a prelude to courting."

"The doctor is not courting me," Loreli said. "No one on the Impulsive is. It would require special dispensation from the captain for me, as a ship's sexy, to have a romance."

"That doesn't bother you?" Chi Nikki Chawa asked.

"My work is important to me," Loreli answered, "and my kind, Botanicals, are able to absorb the admiration of others to sustain our emotional health, much in the same way we absorb sunlight for our physical well-being."

"Do you get a lot of sunlight living on the ship?" Chi Nikki Chawa looked at the mild, recessed lighting of the hallway with skepticism.

"The artificial lights are designed to mimic the UV range of Earth's sun. It is sufficient. Still, nothing compares to the power of summer's day."

"You could say the same about love," Chi Nikki Chawa said, and Enigo shrugged to show he agreed.

When they got to the teleporter room, the door would not open.

"Go to Minion Werl at the engineering teleporter," Dour said through the intercom. "My mistress requires privacy."

"Speaking of love..." Chi Nikki Chawa started, but Enigo cut him off.

"It's not like that. His 'mistress,' is the teleporter, and it's like a slave/acolyte thing.

Bizarro. He's probably still doing that freaky ritual of his."

"He's usually faster about it," Loreli added.

"I'll bet he stopped to write a poem or a tragic, depressing song. Next talent night is going to be a hoot," Enigo concluded. His frown and roll of his eyes said what he thought about Dour's idea of entertainment.

Chi Nikki Chawa shook his head. "Despite my evolved intellect and the assistance of your ship's translators, I am still not sure I understand."

"Don't worry about it. Nobody understands Dour. He likes it that way."

In the teleporter room, Teleporter Chief Dolfrick Dour had indeed finished his poem and his "freaky ritual," but was pondering the portents his mistress had laid before him. Today, he had destroyed and rebuilt the physical vessels of four souls: an alien, a human woman, and two human brothers...

Two brothers, at least. He wasn't quite sure one was fully human.

* * *

Enigo ended up carrying the scanner, after all. He'd decided his own chivalry wouldn't let Loreli carry it, and the doctor had insisted that since Enigo was so qualified at waving the blue glowy wand, he could do that while the doctor conducted more mundane physical examinations.

"Besides," Dr. Pasteur added, "once we explained what we were doing at the battlefield, the natives were more peaceful and cooperative than the humans. I don't think we're in any danger." Chi Nikki Chawa had agreed.

Enigo shifted under the straps and held back a sigh. He didn't usually regret the bar fight that had led to his punishment detail working with the sensor wand, but days like today, he wished he'd behaved better at the Academy.

Loreli nudged him with her elbow and grinned at him in amusement and sympathy. He grinned back. Over the past couple of adventures, their friendship had grown. He didn't need anyone to "get" him, but it was nice to think someone did. Not to mention, he loved the way her hair reacted to the sun.

They'd materialized and met the doctor in a small clearing not far from the village to go the rest of the way on foot. Chi Nikki Chawa had not wanted to frighten any of his people with the teleporter.

They walked along a trail between two cultivated fields just starting to sprout some kind of gourd. Before them was the village, a neat array of mud huts with thatched roofs, their wood doors open for the breeze but the entries covered with beautiful, colorful blankets that gave them privacy. To the left, a large clearing served as a workplace. Food was cooking over fires or roasting in coals, watched over by maidens instructed by older women. The elderly shucked vegetables and called out warnings to the children rushing about in a game of tag. In all, it was the idealized kind of primitive town that would show up on an internet meme with a caption saying such people have no need for roads, money, schools, or hospitals...and thus are the natural prey for an Evil Civilization ™ such as that which the Lone Star represented.

When they got within sight, however, all activity paused while the villagers took in their strange new visitors.

Then a child exclaimed, "Ti Chini Tawsi!" and all the little ones ran to Loreli, squealing and demanding to touch her.

Chi Nikki Chawa held Enigo back with a friendly arm. "I should have thought of this. Loreli, with her green skin and plant-like hair, looks like a character from one of our favorite children's tales. Ti Chini Tawsi is a ground spirit who teaches respect for the land and all creatures in it."

One of the children toddled to her, carrying a gourd almost as big as he was and filled with water which spilled from the rim with each step. When he got to her, he upended the entire thing at her feet.

"No!" Chi Nikki Chawa shouted too late.

Loreli gasped as the cool water hit her, soaking her from knees to toes.

Enigo burst out laughing.

"Enigo!" Loreli protested, though she was grinning at the child, who with confusion looked from Chi Nikki Chawa's stern frown to the alien stranger half bent in laughter.

"Lieutenant!" the doctor chided. "Why didn't you stop him?"

"Oh, sorry, Doc. All this equipment on my back, made me hesitate. I didn't want to get it wet. Besides, I think this means Loreli, at least, has been accepted."

The doctor's glare said he didn't buy that excuse, but of course, he said nothing. Being mild and unobtrusive was Guy Pasteur's fallback position for most things. It made him easy to work with, but not an especially standout character, which is why...

Sorry—spoilers.

In fact, their reaction did seem to satisfy the hesitant watchers-on, and soon the whole village was gathering around them. Even as his guffaws mellowed to snickers, however, Enigo kept a wary eye on the growing crowd. Chi Nikki Chawa explained the three and their mission.

As he did, Loreli said to Enigo. "Perhaps I should ask them to water you?" She squatted and held her hands out to the boy. He placed the jug in them. Rather than flinging the remaining water at the chief of security, she turned it around in her hands, admiring the carvings. "This is beautiful."

Chi Nikki Chawa said, "My people—or rather, those that were my people—do not have the technological advancement nor the desire for many luxuries, but beauty has always been important to us. We try to make every creation, no matter how practical, a work of art."

"Speaking of art…" Enigo's mirth had completely faded, and he focused a frankly admiring stare at a young, wild-eyed woman who was sidling between people toward them.

"Enigo! What has gotten into you?" Loreli protested. She, too, looked up at the woman who was beautiful and nubile and covered in some simple strips of fabric over skin-tight clothing of intricate designs.

"No, I mean her skin. It's awesome."

Loreli looked again, and saw that what she'd mistaken for a bodysuit was actually the woman's skin, fully covered in tattoos.

Chi Nikki Chawa explained, "That's Ta Pala Chawa, my cousin. She carries our generation's history in the art upon her body."

"Wikadas!"

The woman seemed equally fascinated by Enigo. She pushed through the last of the adults barring her way and hurried to him. She took hold of the hand he'd been using to point at her, and traced the letters tattooed on his knuckles.

"Like those?" he asked. "I got them when I was twelve, preparing for the Fight for the Grand Auditorium. We'd agreed fists only, so I wanted to be prepared to bring the pain and fear. See? Pain —" He mocked a punch with his left. "- and Fear." He described an uppercut with his right.

The universal translator did its job, and she nodded appreciatively. "A warrior. More?"

"*Spuestokay!* Lemme show you my phoenix. That was a revenge fight. Got stabbed four times, so it covers the scars. See?" He started to pull up his shirt.

"Enigo!" Loreli cut in sharply. "We have limited time to conduct our studies and report back to the captain."

The doctor totally missed the uncharacteristically frantic tone in Loreli's voice but did decide this was a good time to take charge. "Quite right, Loreli. Chi Nikki Chawa, is there somewhere more private where we can conduct the scans? Away from the crowds, at least?"

Ta Pala Chawa had hold of Enigo's "fear" hand and was pulling him into the village.

Chi Nikki Chawa shrugged. "It seems Ta Pala Chawa will show you a hut you may use. Meanwhile, Doctor, with your permission, I will escort Loreli to our elders' meeting place. We can then explain the situation where she can see it for herself."

The doctor clapped his hands together once. "Excellent. Divide and conquer. We'll get more done that way. Loreli, please report at regular intervals."

And with that, the Botanical xenologist was led away by their Evolved Paleo guide and surrounded by Paleo children while Enigo skipped off hand-in-hand with the beautiful stranger, the doctor following in his wake like a rogue branch that needed pruning.

Loreli shook herself mentally. Could the air of this strange planet be filling her head with such thoughts? Whatever this envy she was feeling meant, she needed to set it aside and concentrate on her job.

* * *

Captain's Log, Intergalactic Date 676889.86

As we await the data gathered by my away team, I have decided it was best to give my cousins a little cool-down time. We've placed them in adjoining quarters, so Bobby could freshen up, and J.R. and Sue Ellen could discuss whatever was eating them. In the meantime, I've set my engineering and ops departments to figure out how we can safely tow the Lone Star home. I want us to be able to take action if we find it prudent to leave quickly.

One of the best parts of being a HuFleet Captain is the ability to tell my people, "Figure it out, and report to me." Times like these, it's vital. I'm thrust into the role of diplomat and counselor, and even though I don't know these distant cousins personally much, it's all the harder for them being family.

Captain Tiberius entered the guest quarters he'd assigned to J.R. and Sue Ellen. From the moment Minion O'Tin had registered the security alert on the bridge, Jeb had regretted giving the couple privacy to work things out. At least he had left the security team outside their door. Those two had rushed in to pull J.R. off his wife, whom he was choking, and then two more had to be called in to stop Sue Ellen from attacking them. Jeb stepped in to hear profanities and excuses being shouted at top volume.

As soon as J.R. saw him, the man's face took on an even deeper shade of rage red. He lunged toward the captain, but the guards held him tight. LaFuentes had trained them well.

"Jimmy Ray, you may be my cousin, but keep this up and I'll call your momma."

"Leave her out of this!"

"Then calm yerself down. I am downright shocked at such behavior, especially from a Seip. We don't beat our women, not in this century and not three hundred years ago, either."

"And we don't steal each other's women, especially from family. How dare you seduce my wife?"

Sue Ellen cut in. "I tried to tell him it was just a squeeze of the butt. It was a religious experience."

"Oh, right! You used to say that about us."

Jeb sighed. Well, he knew that evangelization had its pitfalls as well as its perks. "In this case, cousin, it's literal. Observe. Minion Brahe?"

Minion Brahe checked to ensure Sue Ellen was calm, but that his partner had a good grip on her, anyway. Then he went to join the captain for a demonstration of their faith. There were only four other followers of Keptar on the Impulsive, so it was a remarkable coincidence that they happened to get so much screen time. It has nothing to do with diversity quotas or plot machinations, just happy happenstance, to be sure.

"Kra Keptar, Captain!"

"Fruliogri Kra, Brahe."

They slapped their own butts, then squeezed each other's. This time, however, they retained their grips while the captain intoned, "Great Keptar, who expelled the first gasses that created our amazing universe, may peace and understanding surround this couple like a fog. Bless those who dealt it regardless of whether they smelt it. Kra Keptar."

"Fruliogri Kra!"

Brahe returned to Sue Ellen's side, but she, at least, had calmed down, and in fact, had placed her own hands on her round derriere. Of course, the placement was all wrong, not to mention the way she rubbed her cheeks made Jeb vow to get the ship—and himself—some shore leave, and soon.

He pushed the thought aside, and turned to J.R. "See? Actual religion, albeit alien. I can squeeze yours now if you'd like to ask for forgiveness."

His cousin gaped at him. "You've all gone mad! That was praying? 'Kar Keptar,' my ass!"

"*Kra* Keptar—and it's everyone's asses whether they believe or not. Sue Ellen, for your safety and so that my security crew can get back to their jobs, I'm going to have to move you to another room. Brahe, make it happen and have Sickbay send someone to take care of her bruise. J.R., you're confined to this one until you calm down enough to apologize, and if you raise a stink, I will call your mother. Kra Keptar."

"Fruliogri Kra!" Brahe called out, but Jeb had already spun and left the room, ignoring J.R.'s protests. His away team had better find some answers, and soon. He was already getting tired of his family.

"Captain! Jeb!"

He pulled up short. Figures. He made a short prayer that she would not throw herself into his arms, pasted on a neutral but gentlemanly smile, and turned back to his cousin.

She stopped two respectable steps in front of him. Prayers answered.

"Jeb, don't be too hard on him. I don't know what's gotten into him. I mean, J.R. has always been jealous, but never violent."

Jeb cocked a brow. Seemed his security team would disagree.

She caught his unspoken meaning. "To me, I mean. I've never seen him like this. He's usually so charming, especially with people he needs to influence. But today, he's practically barbaric. It must be the stress, or maybe he got hit in the head... I'll go quietly to my room, now. Don't judge him too harshly."

Jeb watched as she meekly followed Brahe to a new room, but his mind was on the angry cousin he'd just left. Maybe he would talk to J.R.'s mom after all. Sue Ellen could be a woman defending her man, but she could also be right that this wasn't his usual behavior.

And if that was so, something on that planet changed him. And that meant Jeb's people were in danger, too.

Jeb decided to compromise by talking to Bobby first. The younger Seip brother opened the door in a bathrobe, his hair wet and a towel around his shoulders.

"Showers!" he exclaimed like a child discovering an exciting new pastime. "I'd only read about them in the history books. All this luxury—and abundant water, too!"

"Glad you're enjoying the showers," Jeb said drily as the author took a risk of having this sentence bandied about in one of those "You won't believe what these high school students wrote" memes. "I need to talk to you about your brother."

"J.R.? Is he okay?" Bobby stopped rubbing his hair, and there was an edge in his voice that put Jeb on Yellow Alert.

"I just want to know what kind of man he is."

Bobby sighed and sat down on the arm of one of the "luxurious" chairs. "Charming, motivated, super-smart. Also driven, conniving..."

"Violent?"

Bobby rubbed at the bruise still darkening his clean-shaven jaw and smiled wryly.

"Wife beater?"

Bobby jumped up so fast, the towel fell off his shoulders. (Don't get too excited. He had a robe on.) "What the—where did that come from?"

"My men just tore him off Sue Ellen."

"Is she all right? Okay. Good." He started to pace. "I... No. I mean, they've had their rows. One time, they woke up the whole corridor...but hit her? That's not like him. Yet... I dunno. Never mind. It's stupid."

The hairs on the back of Jeb's neck rose. He knew what that meant, thanks to the Actuaries.

Nearly a century ago, a Union ship happened upon a planet where the sapient species was on the way to extinction. It wasn't disease or ongoing war but a kind of inward focus and malaise that had caused the population simply to stop reproducing.

The species, dubbed the Actuaries, lived for statistical research and reducing risks. Unfortunately, they'd done such a good job reducing risks that they'd run out of things to study except why their species was too bored to breed. So everyone lived long, secure, and incredibly unmotivated lives.

Then came the Union, and specifically, the human race, who are anything but dull and secure. The Actuaries found new meaning to their lives. After only a few years, they also realized it would take generations to figure out humans. Their population experienced its first baby boom and has been thriving since.

What's this got to do with Jeb's neck hairs, you ask? Well, one of the most useful studies the Actuaries have done was of every disaster ever to disable or to destroy a human starship. They then came up with the common warning signs that every major calamity had in common—from alien invasion to unidentified virus. On that list was someone on the ship or away team declaring any version of, "Never mind. This is stupid."

Jeb cleared his throat. "Why don't you let me be the judge of that?"

"No, seriously, it can't mean anything. Probably my imagination."

Jeb sighed. Statements Number 4 and 7 on the "likely indicators of starship crisis" list. Every first-year cadet knew that if you were having such thoughts, you went to the doctor, the chief of security or the captain and you did not hold back on the details. "We're family. Humor me."

"Well, when I first saw him, he seemed like he was slouching. J.R. never slouches. I thought I was mistaken, but then when we were walking to our quarters, he was walking funny, too. Now, you tell me he was violent. I dunno. Maybe he was hit in the head?"

Could a concussion turn someone into a maniacal, superpowered, rampaging maniac with hidden knowledge of the ship's systems? It hadn't happened in Jeb's lifetime, anyway.

"Thanks. Why don't you get yourself dressed? I'll have a medic check out J.R."

With a reassuring smile, he left the room. The smile faded to a taciturn but strong expression once the door shut behind him. He tapped his communicator as he strode to the bridge. "Smythe, put the ship on Quiet Yellow and

Intruder Alert. Cut off computer access to our guests' rooms except for the basic Union history files. And have Doall consult the Actuary tables. We may have Four-Seven. I'll be in Sickbay consulting with them."

"Blimey," Smythe swore, and Jeb heard him call out the orders. "Shall I start porting up the Away Teams?"

Dour's voice cut in. "No."

Safely alone in the lazivator, Jeb allowed his frustration to show. "No? Alright, Chief, what's your mistress telling you?"

Dour said, "Her portents are unclear, but we may have an imposter."

* * *

Loreli hesitated in front of the shack where she'd seen that woman drag Enigo, and from which he had yet to emerge. It'd been an hour already; she'd kept track, even as the elders had fawned over her and the children had entertained her with a play. Charming as they'd been, she'd found herself distracted by Enigo's absence, and not because he had the scanning device. That had been left at the door, and the doctor had retrieved it without comment and been taking scans ever since.

In fact, Loreli didn't know why his absence disturbed her so, or why she'd thought of Ta Pala Chawa as *that woman*. Regardless, she was a member of the Impulsive, so as soon as Smythe called, she used the message as an excuse to step away from the festivities. Then, she embraced the spirit for which the ship was named and went to drag Enigo's sorry—er, investigate the reason for his absence.

Now, however, she was feeling just a little stupid and embarrassed—especially when she heard a sharp intake of breath and a small moan come from the tent.

Now, if Loreli had been humanoid (or meat-based)…or if this were a different series… she would either run off to have a self-pitying cry or bang on the door like a jealous lover. But of course, Loreli is a plant, and the ship's sexy, and a xenologist. In other words, a cool professional. So she pushed aside her odd feelings to examine later and knocked calmly on the threshold.

There was a yelp and a thud, and some shuffling. Then Enigo lifted the fabric covering the doorway aside. He did not have a shirt on, and there was a redness on his bicep and chest that he protected with his other hand.

"Fronds! I thought you were interviewing the people. Never mind, get in here. We were just finishing up. You'll want to see this."

Loreli blinked. Had whatever affected the Paleos and J.R. affected Enigo? "Are you all right?"

He glanced at his hand and whatever it hid. "This? I've had worse, but I don't think I'll ever have better. Now get in here. You have to see this. Ta Pala Chawa is some kind of wikadas contortionist..."

"What are you talking about?" she burst out, wondering if she was in some kind of alternate universe "shipping" episode.

Enigo squinted at her. "The tatts. Loreli, I'm fine, okay? Look."

He pulled his hand away to reveal a complex pattern of dark lines that covered the inner front of his arm and pectoral. The area around it was red. She looked behind him into the tent. Ta Pala Chawa sat on a bench, but there were also two men holding bowls of ink and needle-thin knives.

One worked on the woman's elbow as she and the other watched her expectantly.

"You're getting a tattoo? Now?"

"Not just any tattoo—the most wikadas tatt of all time. Come on, and I'll explain."

He grabbed her wrist and pulled her into the cabin.

Enigo released Loreli's wrist as soon as she crossed the threshold. The flap of the small shack closed behind her, and she realized this was not someone's residence, but the tribe's equivalent of a tattoo parlor. She was in part fascinated, relieved, and annoyed at her crewmate.

Enigo set himself back on the stool, and the artist set the bowl aside to manipulate his posture and the position of his arm against his side. Enigo said to her, "Pay close attention, now, because this is the important part. See, their written language is muycho subtle. The length of a line can change the tense of a word, and connecting two characters makes a whole new sentence. Show her, Ta Pala."

Ta Pala Chawa held her arm before her so Loreli could see the designs on the arm and back of her hand. She pointed to her wrist. "The tale of Kor Pi Boto. Kor Pi Boto is an ordinary boy. His village is happy and fertile."

She twisted her wrist and bent her hand back slightly so that part of the tattoo was lost in the folds of skin on her wrist. "The village was happy. It is no longer fertile."

"See?" Enigo cut in. "She's giving you the condensed version, but the point is, a little movement, and it changed the words. Ta Pala has incredible muscle control. She can make her forearm ripple! It is the most amazing and baffling thing I've ever seen."

"The children told me about Kor Pi Boto," Loreli said, her eyes examining the change of the letters as Ta Pala continued to move her wrist, fingers, and forearm in the narration of the story. "He was the first to go to the mountain and come back changed."

Ta Pala smiled, "Yes! Change!" She showed Loreli her other forearm.

"Change."

Then, her neck.

"Change!"

"Ta Pala is carrying the history of every person who went to the mountain and came away changed. She's had some of these since she was chosen at five. She's had to train to move each muscle individually and with purpose. But that's not the mindblower. Show her, Ta Pala!"

The woman twisted her hands together and laid them against her right cheek. Then sitting on the floor, she brought her right leg up and pressed it against her arms, knee bent and foot dangling beside her eyebrow. Loreli understood now the contortionist comment, but more than that she found herself captivated by the design the intersecting lines made.

"What is that?"

"That," Enigo said, "is the rise of the Evolved Paleos."

"So, they added new stories?"

Ta Pala Chawa spoke. "No. I move. I see story—story to come."

"So they expected...?"

"...a long line of superhumanoids," Enigo concluded. "In fact, they've saved her entire back for their stories."

The captain needs to know about this, she thought, even as she asked, "So, they are not afraid of the changes their kin share—even the reduced lifespan?"

"Heroes live hard, die young," Enigo concluded, then hissed as the artist poked a sensitive spot. "The heroes come when the village needs them. It's the same for all the villages—and apparently, every history holder can move their bodies to create this same design."

"They expected this, then—predicted it?" She tore her eyes away from the designs to look Ta Pala Chawa in the face. "What do you need such protection from?"

"You," Ta Pala answered.

Enigo added, "And by 'you,' she means 'us'—the Union."

"Protect your people from the Union?" Loreli asked Ta Pala Chawa. "But you didn't even know the Union existed until today."

Enigo cut in, "Bizarro, yeah?"

"Bizarro," Ta Pala agreed. She untwisted herself, then lay on the ground, brought her legs up over her head from behind and crossed her ankles under her chin. With one hand, she pointed at the door. "You tell now, cousin."

Chi Nikki Chawa entered the small room, pulling the doctor with him. The doctor was protesting that he still had people to examine.

"You have waved your wand at my people enough," Chi Nikki Chawa told him. He gave the doctor a firm push toward one corner of the room. The doctor staggered but did not fall, and true to his gentle, unassuming nature, he took a few extra steps as well.

Then, however, he noticed the others. He looked at Enigo suspiciously. "Are you drunk?"

The chief of security scoffed. "Why would you ask that?"

"We're on a new planet, and first thing, you get dragged off by an exotic woman, who is doing some kind of...performance, and you're getting a tattoo."

"*Ai madrio!* I was building a rapport. It was anthropological research."

Loreli replied, with just a hint of a sneer, "That you wear on your body. Doctor, examine him. He may be drugged. Or perhaps something in this village be affecting us the way it's affected J.R.?"

Ta Pala Chawa made an impatient noise.

"Enough!" her cousin ordered. "Doctor, remain where you are. Everything is unfolding according to the plan—except for you, Doctor. We don't know why you're here. But, Green Woman Loreli, from the moment your sacred feet touched our soil, the prophecies began to move to fruition. Your people and those of the Lone Star will be treated kindly—if they acquiesce to our demands and leave."

"But what about you, Chi Nikki Chawa," the doctor protested. "The Evolved Paleos, I mean. You're dying, and it's because of what we humans did to your world. And the scientists of the Lone Star are wrong—you only have a few years, not decades. If I have more time to study the phenomenon, I'm sure I could help you. We could extend your lives."

"Tell them!" Again, Ta Pala grunted, and there was a strain in her tone.

"Loreli, contact your ship and the Lone Star. I would speak to the captains and to J.R., if he will listen to reason. It is time you understood the Prophecy of the Sky Tear and the Age of Heroes."

* * *

Captain Tiberius stormed out of the lazivator. Before Ensign Doall could call out, "Captain on the Bridge," he demanded, "What do you mean, a Logic ship is hailing us from the other side of the anomaly?"

Smythe answered, "The UFS Impartial Brilliance has apparently been diverted from its survey mission and is en route to us—ETA 3.768 hours at the time of their last transmission. They refused to speak to anyone but you, declaring anyone else an inefficient use of resources."

As he took his seat, Jeb grumbled under his breath about Logics and their idea of efficiency, which really meant dealing with the person they thought would help them best, whether talking to the captain of the ship or "commandeering" an off-duty life support engineer who happened to have some spare time and the qualifications they needed.

From the bullpen, one such life-support engineer ducked his head and hoped not to be noticed. Even though it wasn't his fault the Logician ship UFS Energetic Efficiency had transported him to their engineering section without consulting the Impulsive's chain of command, he preferred to remain unnoticed by either captain. No point in tempting fate.

From the command chair, Jeb took a calming breath and signaled Doall to open comms to the Impartial Brilliance.

"This is Captain Jebediah Tiberius. Make it quick; we're busy."

The view of the planet on the screen changed to the cool modern colors and lens flare of the Logic ship. Jeb never understood the lens flare effect; he knew Logicis had second eyelids against glare, an evolutionary adaptation of living on a desert planet, but why install the effect in their ship? Secretly, he suspected it was to flaunt their anatomical superiority. Logics weren't especially emotional, but they had egos.

This captain was no less so. He raised a single pointed eyebrow and replied, "Indeed you are, Captain Tiberius. The Union received a most interesting communication from your ship—a James Ray Seip who wishes to sell us liquid unobtanium in return for control of the planet which you currently orbit."

Dammit, Jeb thought, apparently a concussion can turn you into a superpowered, raging megalomaniac with a ridiculous knowledge of the ship's systems.

The Logic captain continued, "We've read your status reports. Having been at the aforementioned planet no less than four hours, you have stunned over 200 humans and natives, placed your ship in the direct line of fire between two warring factions—both human according to reports—have allowed a potential intruder aboard, and are dealing with what the Actuaries dubbed a 'Four-Seven.' And, by no means least, uncovered an environmental disaster that could mean the genocide of a species. Have I missed anything?"

"Just that we stopped a civil war, no one has been killed, the four-seven is being handled, and our teleporter chief was overreacting to some anomalous readings, which could be due to the environmental phenomenon. Not disaster. The most current readings sent back from our team on the planet show that to be locally contained and something the natives are long familiar with."

"Be that as it may, we have been dispatched to assist you before this phenomenon becomes a disaster. Have you verified that the liquid unobtanium is indeed the cause of the genetic anomalies?"

On the lower corner of the screen, Doall flashed the answer so the captain could read it without ever looking like he was consulting an underling. "We haven't proven a direct correlation, but it's definitely the key factor."

"Excellent. We've received copies of your scans, and since the unobtanium is located in only a few concentrations around the planet, it will be a simple matter of teleporting it into our freight chambers and replacing it with a natural, inert material."

The Impulsive bridge crew gaped stupidly at the viewscreen, but except for the life-support specialist who was still worrying about getting noticed, they all understood what the Logics captain was implying. The Union planned to steal the Paleos' unobtanium!

Captain Tiberius leaned forward in his seat, one hand up. "Whoa! You can't do that. It doesn't belong to us."

The Logics captain simply raised another eyebrow, the most emotion one of his kind was allowed to display. "It is a dangerous substance that is interfering with the natural development of the indigenous peoples. Your own species has already exploited the natives in order to gain advantage, to the detriment of the species, it seems. Now that this James has broadcast the presence of such a highly valuable substance to this sector, other species will likewise interfere with this world. The most logical course is to remove the temptation. It is for their own protection."

"Their own protection? Look, we're getting the Lone Star out of here."

The captain, who never felt it efficient to share his name, tilted his head as if Jebediah were a slow-witted child. "Indeed—and what of the next ships to seek this most rare fuel? Will you be here to protect them against the Thaggun? Or perhaps the Cybers?"

"You can't steal their resources!"

"Of course not. We shall remove this danger, and in return, we shall offer gentle guidance and assistance in accordance with their evolutionary capabilities."

"Now, hold on. That's interference—you can't do that."

"You humans already have. We are merely striving to heal the damage in the most effective way possible. We shall be in orbit in 3.51 hours. Please have all humans back aboard their ships and the unobtanium mines and processing stations evacuated. Impartial Brilliance out."

"Well, that's just great," Jeb sighed after the screen went dark.

From Ops, Doall said, "I'm sorry, Captain. I did cut off everything as soon as we went to Quiet Yellow. He must have sent the message before that."

"No one was expecting it. All right, people, we have three and a half hours to figure this out. Bridge to Dour—are those teleporters cleared for use yet?"

For once, the teleporter chief spoke without mystic analogies. "I would prefer to keep Room One offline, but the others are functioning."

"Good enough. Work with Gel to coordinate the return of our people, but wait for my go-ahead. Sickbay, what's the deal on J.R.?"

A nurse's frazzled voice answered, "He's been a difficult patient, but Chief Dour is correct—his DNA is altered—slightly, but enough to increase his aggression as well as his intelligence. I've used a neural inhibitor, twice, but he keeps tearing it off. I finally had to sedate him."

"Is he conscious?"

"Does he have to be?"

"That bad? I need him coherent, but we'll send extra security. Gel, have him and his brother Bobby brought to the ready room." He checked to see that Gel was making the arrangements, then turned back to Ensign Doall, "Ensign, contact the Lone Star. They need to know this. And get Lieutenant LaFuentes or Loreli on the line. We may need to talk to Chi Nikki Chawa."

"Actually, Captain, they're hailing us—and Chawa is demanding we leave the planet as well."

Captain Tiberius hadn't had a situation make him want to sputter since his first command on the HMB Whaddahel, but Doall's announcement got him close. He folded his hands together and clenched his glutes in a prayer for strength, then said in a calm and commanding voice, "Well, that's both fortuitous and perplexing. Put them on screen."

Soon, the bridge of the Lone Star was on part of the screen. Donna Bel seemed to be volunteering to take command for a spell. She sat in the command chair doing some knitting. "Captain?"

"Ma'am. We have a situation. Is the First Officer there?"

"Here." He walked from off screen, but motioned for D.B. to keep her seat.

"Excellent. Stand by while we get everyone on the line. We need to make some plans. Ensign?"

On another part of the viewscreen, the deceptively peaceful view of the planet was again replaced with an interior—this time, of a rough hut of hard-packed earth, fabric-covered walls and a thatched roof. While Chawa stood in the foreground, he did not command attention. Rather, the crew's eyes were drawn to the young native who was twisted into a pretzel and looking rather annoyed about it, a stern-faced Loreli, and Enigo sitting calmly in a chair while a native…

"Lieutenant," Jeb asked, "are you getting a tattoo?"

"Yes, he is," Loreli answered, with more barbs in her tone than Jeb had heard since her prickly teenage years.

Enigo rolled his eyes, "I keep trying to explain…"

"Save it for when you're back on the ship. Chi Nikki Chawa, I understand you want all us humans off your planet, and I have no problem with that, but there is a bigger situation you need to know about."

"We already know," Chi Nikki Chawa said, gesturing to the girl. "It has been written in prophecy."

Jeb eyed the girl. "'Written'? On her, you mean?"

The girl wiggled her toes in reply.

"Well, by Keptar's Dimple, man, read it before she gets a cramp."

"Thank you!" The girl spoke for the first time. Then, she lifted one arm to point to where the designs from her ankle intersected with those on the curve of her jaw.

Chawa grimaced at losing his dramatic moment, then intoned, "…and so the ranks of heroes shall swell. A sign shall come. Green

Woman and her...companion...shall arrive from the Beyond. The children will bless her with water. It will be for a sign of the danger to come from the Beyond. They who will threaten The Source and future of the People. Heed then, the plan of the heroes, for they will return the world to the safety and comfort of isolation. Thus, shall the People continue to live in peace and harmony long after the heroes have gone."

"Okay, that's both accurate and vague," Jeb replied as the girl untied herself with katt-like grace. On the bridge, the ready room doors slid open and J.R. and Bobby stepped out.

Jeb continued, "And, on behalf of Green Woman and the rest of crew of the Impulsive, we're glad to return you to your safety and comfort. But this has gone beyond whether or not we should leave y'all alone to die of the unnatural causes we created. My side of the universe knows about your unobtanium, and they're coming for it."

Chawa smirked, "From the time I, the first Evolved Paleo, understood the value you place upon the Source, I and the other heroes like me have been taking secret steps to deny you your prize. We give you three hours to gather your people and leave to where you came. Then, we shall destroy the gateway that let you enter our space."

"Gateway? The anomaly? You can do that? We can't even do that."

Chawa answered with a smug grin and a snort. That arrogance was enough for Jeb. He glanced at First Officer Smythe, who with a nod, started transmitting orders to evacuate.

Suddenly, J.R. stepped forward with a shout. "Traitor!"

The security guards, who allowed the Seips to enter the bridge on condition they behaved themselves, lunged forward and grabbed J.R. by the arms before he could do more than shout. But shout, he continued to do.

"Chawa, you traitorous fornian! I made you what you are. You cannot take this away from me."

Chawa gave the frothing human a pitying look. "I am sorry, J.R., for what I did to you. We were friends once." Then, he turned his attention back to the captain of the Impulsive. "Captain Seip-Tiberius, as we have spoken, others of my kind have been setting plans in motion. Please ensure all humans are upon the ships, but take Green Woman Loreli and her companion—"

From off-screen, the doctor cleared his throat.

"—companions last. They will, as you say, explain when they return to the ship. You must be on the other side of the gateway in two and three-quarter hours."

Chawa's side of the screen went dark.

"Friends?" J.R. surged forward, but Gel had chosen two heavy-worlders for his "escort." They didn't budge. "They promised me—us—me!"

"Billy," he yelled to the First Officer of the Lone Star, "don't you dare recall our people. You tell them to go take that refinery, you hear? That world is ours. We were going to make it ours—it was my legacy!"

"What's gotten into you?" Bobby demanded. On the viewscreen, their mother had put aside her yarn and moved toward the camera.

"J.R., honey. We just want to get home, remember? Back to the Texas great-grandpa talked about?"

"Screw Texas!"

There was a collective gasp on the bridge of the Lone Star, from Bobby, and from Impulsive's captain.

"You'd better take that back, boy," Jebediah said.

J.R. snarled at him, then yelled, "Lone Star, enact James Ray Protocol Alamo—password Rise2-23-18-36Fall3-6-18-36."

For a moment, they saw the confused faces of the Lone Star bridge crew; then the communications cut off.

"Protocol Alamo?" Bobby said, "What the hell is that?"

Doall answered, "Captain, the Lone Star is powering up all its weapons—lasers to maximum, torpedo bays opening. It's aiming for the villages!"

Jeb said, "Cruz!"

The navigator's hands were already flying over his console, "Already moving between. This is going to get bumpy."

The ship shook from the impact of the first barrage against its shields before they could call for Red Alert.

Again, the ship shook as two torpedoes struck the shields.

It should be noted that there's really no reason for the ship to shudder at this point, since the shields are separated from the hull by several kilometers. However, it was discovered early in space warfare that humans needed tactile reminders of the danger they were in if they were going to display a proper level of urgency. Therefore, the inertial dampeners had been tied to react to the shields, translating the punishment they were taking into punishment for the crew. In fact, on some HuFleet ships, a particularly close call could even cause equipment short circuit in a shower of sparks and a chair to eject its occupant over a console.

Jeb's first command upon taking charge of the HMB Impulsive was to have Engineering disable those last two "features," but he kept the inertial rattler tie-in. A good jostling kept the crew on its toes.

"Shields are holding at 98 percent," Minion Gel reported from the Security station. "Shall I shoot back?"

"No!" Bobby cried, then rounded on his brother. "J.R., take it back. Those are our people."

"Ha!" J.R. replied. "You stopped being 'my people,' when you betrayed me. It's too late now, anyway. The communications on the Lone Star are disabled and the ship has only one mission—to fight to glorious death. Yeehaw—mmmph!"

Minion Francisco Tank Martinez clamped a meaty hand over J.R.'s mouth. "You shut up now. Let the captain do his job."

The two staggered slightly along with everyone standing as another barrage hit the wikadas shields.

"Ninety-five percent," Gel reported, sounding bored. It was for J.R.'s benefit, of course. In fact, he was already plotting the time of failure for the shields which, if they followed the usual plot conventions, would decrease exponentially.

"Take J.R. to Sickbay," the captain ordered. Once the doors closed behind his cousin and the two security guards, he called Sickbay. "Medical, we're delivering your patient back to you. Stick him in a paralysis field but keep him conscious. I may need him later. And contact the doctor and tell him Chawa may know something about what's made my kin into an overambitious megamind.

"Doall, do we have comms with the Lone Star yet?"

"I'm trying all frequencies, sir, as well as their shuttle and private comms. Anything with Lone Star technology is locked down. We still have comms with our people, though. If Captain Seip would like to deliver a message, we can relay it."

"Good idea, Doall. Bobby?" Jeb motioned for the younger Seip to join him, then waved to the screen where the computer had designed an impressive in-your-face extrapolation of the Lone Star firing yet another round of lasers. By now the barrage had grown so steady, the ship would be shuddering regularly, so the inertial rattlers had defaulted to a random pattern of ship-shaking designed to keep the crew on its toes when not falling on their rumps.

"How long can the Lone Star keep that up?"

"The weapons are powered by unobtanium. I'm sure my crew is doing everything they can to stop this mess, but J.R. was our computer systems expert."

"So longer than the deadline the Paleos set. Great. Commander Smythe, we're going to bring everyone up here."

"Of course, Captain. I believe Spillover Three should hold everyone until the doctor can clear them from any genetic manipulations."

Jeb loved that he didn't have to think of everything. "Excellent. Get to it. Gel, we're going to give the Lone Star a chance to get control of their ship, but when our shields get to 70 percent, I want you to take out their weapons and whatever else you need to. We can send over medical teams and tow them home if necessary. Sorry, Bobby, but if Chawa and his people have half the technical genius J.R. displayed on this ship..."

Bobby sighed. "I understand, Captain. I'll tell my folks on the ground to give you their complete cooperation."

An ensign from the bullpen stepped up then and led Captain Seip to the ready room where he could send a message to his people on the planet. As she passed by her fellow second-shifters, she gave them a grin and a thumbs-up. Doall has tasked her with a duty—and no one had had to die for it to happen!

* * *

Captain's Log, Intergalactic Date 676889.91

It's been over two hours since Chawa's ultimatum. All of the Lone Star crew have been removed from the unobtanium plant by the Evolved Paleos, and a force shield now surrounds the compound. Using our teleporters and the Lone Star shuttles, we've evacuated most of the humans to the Impulsive. The doctor is checking everyone out for any genetic alterations; so far, only J.R. appears to have been affected. The villagers are holding Lieutenant LaFuentes for training, whatever that means, but Chawa requested it with a promise to return him in enough time for us to warp away, and it's in our best interests to keep him feeling friendly.

Loreli has stayed behind as well to try to talk Chawa into giving us more time to deal with the Lone Star. However, we are also on our own deadline. The Impartial Brilliance is not heeding our warnings and will be this sector of space in 42.75 minutes. Their captain does not believe the Paleos have threatened to close the anomaly; apparently, the more logical explanation is that I'm a [expletive redacted] liar. [Expletive redacted] [Expletive redacted] [Expletive redacted]. We're hoping that if they see us high-tailing it in the other direction, they'll take the Paleos' threat seriously.

We've still not been able to communicate with the crew on board the Lone Star, and the ship continues to fire upon us. When our shields hit 70 percent, Minion Gel began firing back as ordered. We've seen no effect on the Lone Star's shields, however. Bobby says they're powered by the unobtanium generator as well.

Long story short: We can no longer wait for the Lone Star to solve its own problem. We need to disable it and tow it back to the Union side of the universe or abandon it altogether. And we have about 15 minutes to do it.

Jeb clicked off the recording and spun his chair to look at the Ops and Security station. "So, what's our status?"

Minion Gel reported, "We've been hitting one spot with a heavy barrage. Engineering reports it's ready to channel a point laser through the deflector dish. That should drill an opening in their shields."

Doall said, "Captain Seip is in Teleporter Room Two. He's ready with the computer virus we've made to force the Lone Star's main computer into a full ship-wide reboot. That will give the crew five minutes to disable their weapons..."

"Otherwise, we'll take them out," Gel said. He said that last in an accent surprisingly reminiscent of his boss.

"Captain Seip also has an EMP grenade in case he can't get the virus to work, and we have a Logic Cyberblaster torpedoes to teleport through as a third option. It didn't work on the Cybers, but the Lone Star's computers are more primitive."

Jeb gave them both approving nods, then said, "Captain to shuttle bays. Y'all ready to launch?"

The shuttle bay coordinator answered, "Yes, sir. As soon as the Lone Star shields are down, we'll get in close. If they have problems getting the ship back online, we're ready to receive their shuttles and escape pods as well as use our teleporters and bring in whatever children we detect."

"Excellent. Teleporter rooms? Chief Dour, are you ready?"

The Teleporter Chief intoned, "The tributes have been prepared, and my mistress shall spin them to thread and pass them through the eye of the needle and reweave them upon their destination."

In the background, they heard Bobby Seip ask, "Uh...Is that safe?"

"It will be swift and painless."

Jeb suppressed a chuckle. "You're in good hands, Bobby. On Doall's mark, then. All right, people, let's get to it!"

Just because they only had 15 minutes left to solve the problem, didn't mean they hadn't been working on it for the past two hours.

"Mark," Doall said.

"Point laser firing," a voice in Engineering replied.

They heard a whine as the ship simulated the effort of channeling light energy into the deflector to fire in a thin ray at the Lone Star's shields.

Then, the sound died.

The viewscreen went blank.

The ship became eerily still.

"Teleporter room," Doall said, "we've pierced the field, send Captain Seip through."

"Are you sure?" Dour asked.

"Do it!"

Meanwhile, Jebediah demanded a system's status on the Impulsive.

"Sair!" Chief Engineer Deary said, "We're experiencing a cascade failure of the special effects algorithms."

"Oshittno." The captain voiced the thought of everyone on the bridge.

"Aye, sair. The backups, too. I can't even pull up bagpipe music, let alone Wagner. It looks like sabotage."

"Captain," Minion Gel interrupted from the Security and Weapons station, "Lone Star just struck us with five torpedoes. Shields at 20 percent."

Around the bridge, a few people exchanged glances and shrugs.

"Look alive, people!" Smythe ordered. Immediately, station heads reported the impact to their departments while the second-string crew in the bullpen threw themselves to the ground to create a sense of drama.

The First Officer nodded approvingly, then asked the captain, "You don't think J.R...?"

Jeb's scowl said that was exactly what he thought. "This time, he's underestimated us. We'll deal with the sabotage later. We have a mission to finish. Computer, this is Captain Jebediah Tiberius of the HMB Impulsive. Activate Improv Sequence One. Authorization, Code One, One A."

"Computer, this is Commander Phineas Smythe. Improv Sequence two. Code One, One A, Two B."

A sigh from Engineering, then: "Computer, this is Commander Deary, Chief of Engineering. Improv Sequence Three. Code One B, Two B, Three."

Without the special effects, there wasn't even a beeping and flashing of lights to show the computer making its calculations. Instead, a male voice reminiscent of a twentieth-century country rock star said, "Y'all sure about this?"

"Computer, this is Captain Jebediah Tiberius. Set timer for a ten-minute countdown and implement Improv Sequence. Authorization: Zero, Zero, Oshittno, Zero."

"You got it, Captain." The computer's voice grew loud and harsh. "Listen up, apes and gelatins! This is the Impulsive! We got a mission to do and ten minutes to do it in, and slackers are not going to be tolerated. Anybody who lets their reaction times fall below red alert standards is going to get zapped, so you keep your eye on your consoles and head in the game because I ain't spending a week in dry-dock because you didn't take things seriously enough. Is that understood?"

"Yes, Pulsie!" The words echoed off the hallways, but of course, the computer feigned deafness and everyone yelled louder...everyone, of course, except Doall, who was monitoring Captain Seip's progress; the teleporter teams, who were already porting over the non-essential people from the Lone Star; the confused Lone

Star crew; and one guy in sensor operations who hadn't really believed the Oshittno Improv sequence was a real thing. That poor minion got a zap to his behind that he would never forget.

And just in time, too, because what the sensor operator saw on his screen made him yelp almost as loud as the Impulsive's high-voltage motivational goose.

On the Bridge, Doall saw the same thing, "Captain! The Lone Star has fired thrusters and is on a collision course with us!"

* * *

Loreli watched in sympathetic fascination as Chi Nikki Chawa and his cousin continued to torture Enigo.

"No, no, no!" Ta Pala Chawa said. "You flex here!" She poked Enigo on a freshly tattooed spot on his pectoral, just below the armpit.

Enigo winced.

"Yes! Good. Now hold!" She twisted his arm slightly, then pointed at the line that flowed from his chest to his bicep. "No fist! Loreli, see? 'Hero of near past.' Now, fist, Enigo. See? Thick line, 'Hero of far past.'"

"You'd better be getting this," Enigo hissed. His face was red and sweaty from effort and pain, and the complex tattoo that ran down the left quarter of his side and much of his upper arm was tender and swollen from Ta Pala Chawa's prodding and manipulations. This had long since stopped being fun.

"I am, Enigo, and I am recording. Chi Nikki Chawa, if you'd just postpone closing the anomaly, we could take time to learn your language more thoroughly, and with considerably less pain for Enigo."

Chi Nikki Chawa gave her a sympathetic smile. "It is not for me to decide, Leaf Lady. J.R. himself set these happenings into motion when he made us steal the secret of the Mountain for him. But we would have your people know about us. Enigo LaFuentes will carry the stories of our people."

"We could have recorded our cousin."

"Now, you mention this?" Enigo exclaimed, then yelped as Ta Pala Chawa manipulated his arm into an awkward angle.

"See? See? Motion into future," she said. "Enigo, you pay attention."

Chi Nikki Chawa continued, "The Lone Star has, in fact, many recordings of my cousin that I hope they will share, but our history is living, our legends grow—and, as you have seen, the future is foretold in the movements of the history bearers. It is our hope that Enigo LaFuentes will carry this gift as well."

"Whoa! I'm a prophet! So...if I do this, what's my future?" He gave his arm a random twist.

Chi Nikki Chawa started to protest that that wasn't how it worked, but when he saw the pattern of lines, he fell silent. His cousin gave a delighted squeal.

"What? What'm I foretelling?"

At that moment, the communicator chirped with a "Prepare for Teleportation" signal. Chi Nikki Chawa gathered Enigo's shirt and their equipment and thrust them into Loreli's arms. He gave her a gentle push toward Enigo.

"Go! And do not forget us!"

"Hey! What's my arm saying?"

"Be good to each other!" Ta Pala Chawa said as the world around the Enigo and Loreli dissolved. Then, they were in a crowded teleporter room.

"Aw, man!" Enigo whined as the teleporter effect faded, and then the pain and fatigue hit. His knees buckled. Loreli caught him and eased him to a sitting position at the foot of the teleporter pad.

"I'm okay. I'm okay," he muttered. Nonetheless, Loreli continued to support him. It was kind of nice. He let himself lean on her. She smelled like a meadow. He closed his eyes and sighed. He'd started the day with a firefight and ended it in the arms of a beautiful woman—and he had a wikadas new tatt. "This was a good day you know?"

Chief Dour leaned over the console to peer at them. "Are you drunk?"

* * *

Tonio opened his mouth to report his move, but Gel spoke first. "Captain! CompuSec reports a cyberattack originating from Sickbay. Countermeasures in progress."

The engineering officer exclaimed, "Sir! Engines are going offline!"

Suddenly, a voice sounded over the intercom. "Fools! Do you think I'm so easily thwarted?"

"Nurse Bradshaw?" Commander Smythe said.

"What? No! It is I, J.R. I am speaking through this Nurse. He is my puppet now."

"Honest mistake," Smythe said.

The captain groaned. "Oh, come on? You have psychic abilities now? How'd that happen?"

"Like I should tell you... But, then again, why not? Yes, liquid unobtanium is a treasure, but what that mountain did to the Paleos? Imagine if we could do that to already evolved humans! With the help of the Evolved Paleos, I took their secret and made it mine."

"Well, why'd it turn you into a loon instead of nice, peaceable type like the Paleos?" Jeb asked. As he did so, he pointed at Gel, then the vent.

Gel gave a gelatinous equivalent of a nod of understanding. His brain was so completely different from a humanoid that they were psychically incompatible. He waved a pseudopod at the bullpen and the relief Security Officer leaped out of his seat and hurried to the Security console, staggering on the way to demonstrate his sense of urgency. From the bullpen, more than one junior officer sighed admiringly. Gel oozed into the nearest vent.

Meanwhile, J.R.-through-Nurse-Bradshaw snarled. "You insult me? When I can control your ship and your people?"

"It relieves the stress. Look, cousin: I don't want to be stuck here, and I definitely don't want to be killed, so how about you give us our nurse back, take a nap, and let us capture the Lone Star, and we'll discuss this on the other side?"

"I need that mountain! *Humankind* needs that mountain if we are to ascend. If we cannot have it, I will destroy it. Now, give me control of this ship, and together, we can conquer the Paleos and take their secret for ourselves. With both our crews Evolved Humans, then we will conquer the galaxy!"

"I thought you knew the secret," Jeb said.

"Metaphorically, fool! There is something in the atmosphere when mixed with the unobtanium as it is processing—"

Jeb interrupted. "Yeah, right. But I thought you said you control my ship?"

J.R.-through-Bradshaw made an impatient sound. "I meant I could! It would be faster if you'd cooperate. Must I explain everything? Are you truly so dense?"

"Nah, I'm just stalling."

"Stalling? What do you possibly think—glurb!" Over the intercom, they heard gurgles and grunts.

Minion Gel said, "I've got him, sir, but he's fighting me. J.R. has a strong hold on him. I wouldn't let any other humanoids in here."

From Security, the acting bridge officer said, "Activate a Level Five psychic disruption field, sir? It could affect anyone within 20 meters."

"Do it," Jeb said.

"Engines are back online," Engineering said a moment later.

The Impulsive said, "Listen up, apes and other life forms! We got 4 minutes to be on the other side of that breach. Do you want to be stuck here? Because I don't. Move, move, move!"

"Shit! Did the Lone Star impale itself on our shields?"

Lieutenant Cruz said, "*No,* va bene, Capitano. I moved us out of the way and caught it in a tractor beam. Lone Star's engines are still engaged. It's orbiting us, which is making us spin in circles, if anyone wants to feign some dizziness. Problem is, I can't move the Impulsive until we can point the right way."

From Security, the officer said, "The EMP torpedoes! How about if we teleport one into the engines? The blast should knock them out without destroying the ship."

"All right then. Beer me. Bridge to Teleporters. We got all our people?"

"My Mistress has welcomed Loreli and LaFuentes. They were the last."

"Excellent! Loreli, get to Sickbay and knock out my cousin by whatever means necessary.

"Sir?" LaFuentes protested.

"I know, it's your job, but J.R. is has developed mindjacking powers, and Loreli's plant-based brain should be too alien for him. Just, give her your gun and keep back. Dour, send some torpedoes into the Lone Star's engines."

"Are we still under attack?" Dour asked.

"No, but we're tethered to it, and it's spinning us in circles."

"I shall feign dizziness and overcome it to do your bidding."

"No time, just do it."

"Done. I would lean against the console in exhausted relief, but Lieutenant LaFuentes has taken that role."

"Ai!"

Doall said, "Lone Star engines are down, and we have them within our shields. We are being hailed by the Impartial Brilliance. I told them logic dictates they get the hell out of our way."

"Great work! Cruz, get us out of here, maximum warp. Break some speed records. Doall, open comms to Chi Nikki Chawa. Ready? Chawa, we're heading out. Don't suppose you'd give us an extra couple of minutes?"

Chawa replied, "We cannot pause what we have set in motion, but fear not. Prophecy says you will escape."

"Well, I don't know what kind of pretzel that poor girl had to tie herself into to get that, but we'll take it. About J.R...."

"We can only offer regrets. We had thought the Gift of the Mountain would grant him wisdom and kindness. Instead, his cunning and arrogance dominated. We should not have forced the Mountain to reveal its secrets. Farewell."

"Two minutes to the anomaly. Warp Eight and increasing," Cruz reported. In the bullpen, the crewmen were harmonizing a high whine to simulate the strain of the engines.

"Engineering," Smythe said, "Systems status?"

"Ach. We're fine. Tell them to quit their screeching."

"Tractor beam holding," Doall said.

"Almost there!" Cruz announced.

The viewscreen flickered to life to show the anomaly in front of them, growing bigger on the screen. And on the other side, also gaining on the anomaly, was the huge hull of the Impartial Brilliance. It rapidly filled the area of the anomaly.

"Y'all got 60 seconds," the Impulsive said, then started a countdown in an accentless voice.

"Cruz..." the captain said.

"No problem, Capitan. We'll get through before them and I'll slip right past."

"Sir, they are not slowing down," Doall reported. "They'll be caught on this side of the anomaly—or in it as it closes."

The Lazivator doors opened and Lt. LaFuentes strode onto the bridge. The officer at the security console frowned dejectedly and relinquished his station, but the Chief of Security told him, "No, man. You finish this one. I'll watch."

Meanwhile, the captain had muttered something about always having to save their allies. "Sound Red Alert. Wikadas shields full to front. Security, can you make them convex?"

"Uh...."

La Fuentes leaned past his confused subordinate and pointed at the right buttons.

"Yes, sir! Done sir!"

"Good. Cruz, ram that ship's shields."

"Woohoo! Pulsie, more power! Shield impact...now!"

Everyone lurched slightly forward and then back to simulate the impact. Those not doing anything on the bridge started harmonizing a lower hum to imitate the different strain on the shields.

"We're pushing them back," Doall said.

"Captain," Cruz said, dropping his accent, "The effort of pushing them is slowing us down. We'll clear the anomaly, but the Lone Star won't."

Doall said, "I'm on it. Adjusting tractor beam to pull them forward."

"Five seconds!" Pulsie said. (And the narrator actually timed it)

"We're through!" Cruz said.

"Three..."

"Lone Star's through," Doall reported with more calm.

On the screen, the anomaly, once a multicolored tear in the universe, shrunk to a blip and was gone.

The ship's intercoms rang with the voice of the Impulsive. "One! Hell, yeah, apes! You did it! First round's on me!"

A cheer went up on the bridge and indeed, all around the ship. When the Impulsive promised "a round," it usually meant something special on everyone's personal replicator rations. How the ship knew exactly what each person would love would probably be considered creepy, except that after centuries of Alexa-like machines, the human race was used to it.

Doall interrupted, "Captain, we're being hailed by the Impartial Brilliance. Would you like to answer?"

"Why not? Put them on screen."

The stoic face of the Logic captain appeared on the screen. "Captain Tiberius, it would seem you were correct in your assessment of the anomaly's imminent closure. Logic dictates that I thank you for..." His voice trailed off, and his attention focused on the Security station, where Lt. LaFuentes was quietly evaluating his subordinate's performance under pressure.

"Captain," the Logic asked, "why doesn't that man have a shirt?"

* * *

Captain's Log, Intergalactic Date 676890.02

We're back on our side of the galaxy. Systems on the Impulsive are being restored. We're running a complete security sweep for any other "surprises," but with J.R. in a forced coma, we've not had further issues. The Lone Star is still undergoing a system reboot—the updates are taking forever!—and its drives are down thanks to our torpedo, so we are towing it home. Just like a family reunion, I'm telling ya.

Speaking of, there's nothing wrong with life support on the Lone Star, so they're throwing a rip-roaring Homecoming party and cotillion. With all the work to be done, we're partying in shifts. Of course, the command crews of both ships still have a pressing issue to deal with: What to do with my cousin.

The primary officers of the Impulsive sat in the large table in the main conference room. With them were several of the main crew of the Lone Star: Bobby, Sue Ellen, Billy Seip, Donna Bel, and the Lone Star's navigator, general practitioner, and geneticist. The navigator wasn't there for any official reason; he was J.R. and Bobby's younger brother. J.R.'s mother, Donna Bel, sat in the chair Lt. LaFuentes normally occupied. She wrung her hands. Enigo leaned against the wall, trying not to move in any way that caused his arm to touch the fabric of the shirt the captain had insisted he wear. Across from Donna Bel, Loreli cast him the occasional glance, both concerned and befuddled, and skillfully looked away whenever it seemed he might catch her gaze.

At the head of the table, the doctor was pointing to an image of J.R.'s DNA. The usual twisted ladder structure looked oddly overfull in the middle, where nucleobases split at the hydrogen bonds to make base triples instead of base pairs. He flipped to another slide—this one a series of images with different timestamps, marked in months and years.

"So, the same thing that's happening with J.R.'s DNA is what happens to the Evolved Paleos. And as you can see, it increases over time. This one is from someone who was 'chosen' only a few months ago—see how these splits are few and far between? While this one is Chi Nikki Chawa's, which is much more fragmented."

"I concur," the geneticist said from her spot at the table. "We were seeing the same thing. We're certain that's why the Evolved Paleos die so much younger than their peers. They can only take so much fragmentation before their DNA becomes unviable."

Dr. Pasteur flipped slides. "But look at J.R.'s. His is continuing to split and at a far faster rate than the Paleo's. That's why we're seeing the manifestation of such bizarre abilities, like the psychic manipulation of Nurse Bradshaw. He's fine, incidentally, though a little embarrassed at the trouble he caused, particularly in his fight with Minion O'Tin. I think he still has Gel between his teeth."

"How long does my boy have?" Donna Bel asked.

The geneticist sighed and reached out to take her hand. "That's the good news and the bad news."

Dr. Pasteur said, "The good news is his body is adapting to the changes. We're not seeing any cellular decay; far from it. He seems to be enjoying the excellent health and regenerative abilities the Paleos first exhibit, but his are only getting stronger. The bad news is that he's only getting stronger. If we don't find a way to return him to his old self, genetically, he'll evolve beyond humanness. And given the level of arrogance he's already displayed..."

"Uhyanno," LaFuentes cut in. "Sorry, Captain, I know he's family and all, but we're not letting him cross the Mitchell line."

Almost every race that has traveled the galaxy has run into something at one point or another that gives them bizarre, godlike powers. In fact, the Fermi paradox was refined to include the number of alien races that were wiped out by one of their own kind so "gifted." There was even one race where the Supreme One got addicted to cutting the population in half until there was only himself. The only evidence of his existence were legends, half a gauntlet, and the words, "just once more."

Enigo had strict orders and even stricter conditioning to never let anything like that happen to humans. He would disintegrate the evolving man if he had to take the entire ship and himself with them—and if he failed, every security officer on the Impulsive would move in to complete the mission.

Jeb nodded. "Let's not give up just yet. How long do we have?"

Dr. Pasteur shrugged. "He's adapting to our attempts to keep him under. I wouldn't wait more than an hour."

"Options?"

The geneticist answered, "No gene therapy we've tried has worked on the Paleos, much less J.R."

"And I've dosed him with enough imposazine to cure a Trigelian Rex of ghonnoriac leprosy.

Medical science has failed us. His new DNA is simply too adaptable."

"So, we gotta give him his old DNA back?" LaFuentes asked. The doctor, in a rare display of emotion, glared at him like he was an idiot, but the geneticist perked up and snapped her fingers.

"Your teleporters! We can get you a copy of his original DNA, and you know the foreign elements that are infecting him. Let's put him in the teleporter and take out the pathogen that's invaded his DNA and cells."

The doctor sighed. "It doesn't work that way. First, we'd need very recent, complete scans of his system on the thread level."

"Thread?" the geneticist asked.

"Sorry, teleporter theory was developed long after your ship had disappeared. You see, threads are the particles that make up strings that make the quanta that make us all," the doctor explained. "However, it's an amazing amount of data, so the teleporter erases it once it's verified that the person has arrived safely in whatever condition he was found in. It clears the buffers for the next teleport.

"But here's where it gets complex. We know there's a finite amount of matter and energy in the multiverse. Those are defined as the threads, which travel among the universes. Every decision you make, from whether you decide to nod sagely or stare at me with confusion (like you are right now) causes the threads to move into the new universe with you or break away to be replaced with different threads. Enough small decisions—or a few major ones—and you are no longer dealing with the same person on a thread level. The teleporters can't reconcile the differences consistently, and if they don't, you could end up with a completely different person."

"How do you know so much about teleportation and thread theory?" Enigo asked.

"Are you kidding? This is the first class we take at HuFleet medical. Every doctor goes in wanting to miraculously cure their patients using the teleporter. It's a ridiculously stupid idea bordering on malpractice."

Jeb nodded thoughtfully. "So we can cross the Mitchell line—"

"Ain't gonna happen, Captain."

"We can kill a man who happens to be family, or we can try something ridiculously stupid. So... How many decisions before we get another person?"

"You're kidding me, right? No, of course not. This is the Impulsive." Dr. Pasteur sighed, then did as any good HuFleet member did. He told himself, "Screw it. Hold my beer and watch."

Aloud, he said, "Well, in theory, if we had his last teleporter scan and we could just reprogram the DNA, it might be enough. There's a chance of dementia."

"He's already demented," Jeb countered, "At least this way, he won't have godlike powers to go with it."

"He'll at least lose some of his memories. He'll probably experience temporary dizziness, drowsiness, lack of coordination—obviously, he should not fly the ship or operate heavy machinery..."

"He's not going to like that," Bobby muttered.

"...constipation, swelling of the hands and feet, night sweats, halitosis, loss of libido..."

Donna Bel turned to Sue Ellen, "Will you be all right with that?"

She nodded bravely, and Jeb knew she'd cope, particularly since her bare foot was rubbing against his calf.

"...and of course, he'll need regular genetic testing to make sure the condition doesn't reassert itself, and it should go without saying that he should not father any children, which considering the libido loss, probably won't be an issue. But this is all academic, anyway. We don't have his teleporter scan."

"Actually," LaFuentes said, "we may."

* * *

Teleporter Chief Dour had actually gone to the Lone Star cotillion. However, Minion Werl in Teleporter Room Two reported that Dour had just asked for transport back when the captain paged him. Donna Bel and Sue Ellen excused themselves to go to the chapel so they could pray. Jeb watched as Sue Ellen started to pray even as they walked down the corridors. Donna Bel yanked her daughter-in-law's hands off a passing crewman's behind. "Stop that nonsense! We're good Evangelicals, and don't you forget it."

He shook his head, but in his heart, he knew Donna Bel was right; Sue Ellen was not really a believer. She would never progress beyond "culturally Keptarian." He lengthened his stride to catch up to the others. They entered the teleporter room just as the sparkling of the teleportation process was reaching its crescendo.

When it subsided, Dour stood on the teleporter, but not alone. He had his arms around two beautiful women in fancy gowns who in turn clung to him amorously. They gazed at him in wonder.

"And now," he told the buxom brunette who was stroking his lank hair. "You have experienced the nanosecond of death. You are no longer the same woman." To the slight blonde whose right hand was tucked under the lapel of his jacket, he said, "The very threads of your being have been torn asunder, caressed in their ravaged state by the cosmic totality, and refashioned into something...other."

"That is so intense," she breathed and leaned in closer.

Captain Tiberius cleared his throat loudly.

At the sight of Bobby Seip, their own captain, the girls jumped to attention, their faces pink with embarrassment. Dour released the ladies, but he seemed more disappointed than embarrassed.

Jeb smiled with good humor, "At ease, everyone. Our apologies, ladies, but we need my teleporter chief for a spell."

Dour sighed, "What peril are we in that we need the labors of my mistress to survive?"

The ladies, who had brightened at the thought of their date being such a needed hero, darkened at the words, "My mistress." One actually curled her lip in a snarl.

Dour ran a finger along her jawline. "The teleporter is my mistress: generous in her rewards and exacting in her demands."

"Yeah, yeah, he's weirdly dedicated to his work," Enigo said. "But we've got about forty-five minutes to figure out how to rip apart J.R.'s DNA and put him back together as something 'other' or whateverthehell you said, or I gotta go kill him before he's too powerful to stop."

Bobby added, "He was affected by the planet. Now, he's developing superhuman powers—and superhuman arrogance to go with it. He's in a medically-induced coma, and still, he is fighting his way to consciousness. He almost destroyed both our ships. This is the only option."

Enigo shrugged, "But what we'd rather do is use the teleporter to reset his DNA. And I know that as part of your weird teleporter ceremony that you collected his teleporter record as well a gene sample."

"That is twice you have used 'weird' in reference to my vocation," Dour said.

"But is it true?" the blonde asked, again stepping closer.

He, however, pinned his glare upon the group in front of him. "Captain, we are speaking of forbidden arts. And Doctor, you are HuFleet trained; have you not told them?"

Dr. Pasteur threw up his hands in defeat. "Of course, I explained it all—thread theory, the dismal chances of successfully getting their old J.R. back, all the side effects from dementia to blocked bowels, even halitosis. I told them it was impossible."

"It is not impossible, but my mistress could exact a most terrible price."

"So, you can do it?" the brunette asked, setting her hand on Dour's arm.

"I have the materials. I have been initiated into those iniquitous mysteries. What you ask is both great and dreadful." He seemed to shiver, but it was hard to tell if from fear, excitement, or simple theatrics. Regardless, the ladies responded by again moving in close to fawn on him.

"This is really so intense," the blonde breathed into his ear.

"J.R. is a great leader of our people," her brunette friend replied. "If you can save him..."

"He will not be the same."

"Are any of us? I mean, you said I have been made...other."

Dour turned his stern gaze to his captain. "There will be consequences, you understand? We will be forcing my mistress to perform acts unnatural to her design."

Jeb, who by years of leadership experience, was able to hide his mirth and keep a placid, commanding expression, nodded. "I understand, but it is a defining quality of this crew that we push ourselves and our equipment beyond what was previously thought possible. This is one of those occasions—provided, of course, you can make the proper calculations?"

"Can I make the proper calculations?" He rolled his eyes in disdain. Then, with a sudden movement, he held up his palms and shrugged out of the girls' grasps. "Enough! I must begin the preparations. Minion Werl, send a janbot to clean Teleporter Room Four. It must be pristine. I assume we have his complete genetic mapping prior to the inciting incident? I will require it sent to my computer. Doctor, prepare your patient: purge his body of toxins and unnecessary impurities."

"Antibiotics and enemas. I know the drill."

"And brush his teeth. I shall retire to my room where I shall complete the 'proper calculations,'"—he all but sneered the phrase—"and retrieve the materials. We shall reconvene in twenty-five minutes. And, I will need the candles."

"Can we help?" the girls asked anxiously.

His gaze moved over them each, as if judging their worthiness. "You may help me with my robes."

Twenty-seven minutes after Dour's instructions were given, Captain Tiberius led a small group to Teleporter Room Four. The doctor and Bobby carried J.R., who had been dosed with enough sedatives to put an Orion bloodbeast into a coma. The doctor was counting on it lasting about 10 minutes. Just in case, however, LaFuentes followed with his raser set on maximum stun and a second one set to disintegrate. Loreli and Minion O'Tin followed, just in case J.R. gained control of his psychic abilities.

The door slid open to a dim chamber that smelled of antiseptic and paraffin. The teleporter pad was lost in shadows, the console illuminated by candles that lined the back edge. Two were held by black-robed women. The cowls obscured their faces. Dour's own cowl rested on his neck. His fingers danced across the console.

"Why's it so dark in here?" Enigo asked.

Dour did not look as he said, "There can be no active devices in this room save the teleporter itself. Nothing can interfere with my mistress's perception of the matter-energy stream. All devices must be left outside the room. That includes insignia—and, yes, Lieutenant LaFuentes, your rasers."

Minion Werl, similarly robed, approached them, an open box in his hands. With a shrug, the captain pulled off his insignia and dropped it in. The others followed suit with their own devices, but LaFuentes hesitated.

"And if he wakes up?"

"Once the teleportation process has begun, he will be helpless to act. Before then, we shall rely on your weirdly effective defense capabilities."

"Hand-to-hand combat by candlelight? Why not?" He dropped his raser into the box. Werl bowed, closed the lid, and placed the box outside the door. Then he locked it from the inside.

Now, Chief Dour looked up—slowly, theatrically. He made a small motion with his hands and the women hastened to put the candles closer so they illuminated his face.

"What you are about to witness has been attempted only a handful of times in teleportation history, and never under such extreme conditions," he intoned as if reciting a ceremonial text rather than voicing a warning.

"The procedures are delicate, and the union between my mistress and myself must be total and uninterrupted. There shall be no movement, no speech. If you must hum, then harmonize in a minor key and maintain no more than eight tones."

With deliberate slowness, he raised his hand. A single pale finger pointed from the wide black sleeves. "Place the victim on Pad Two. He must remain standing. I will tell you when to release him."

Bobby and the doctor did as ordered, balancing him upright and holding him up by a hand each as they backed off the pad themselves. By a miracle, J.R. remained up.

"Now." Dour said.

They let go.

J.R. not only remained standing, but his head snapped up and his mouth opened to yell.

The candle bearers facing the teleporter started to scream a warning.

"Silence!" Dour thundered, and at that moment, J.R. was caught up in the teleporter beam. He tried to reach though, and in fact, the beam seemed to waver. The sparkle lasted unusually long, and its light cast weird highlights and shadows on the walls.

Enigo clenched his fists and traded a look with his team, who tensed (or in Gel's case, solidified slightly) to show they were ready to spring into action if J.R. somehow escaped containment. Otherwise, no one spoke and no one moved, except to look from J.R., who writhed and shouted silently in the field, and Dour, whose hands handled the controls of the teleporter console, making minor adjustments that were intuitive as much as deductive.

Then, the light faded, the beam ended, and the teleporter pad was empty.

One of the candle bearers gasped softly; the other turned her head. Her cowl slipped revealing a tiara over blond hair; it was one of the women who had come aboard with Dour.

Dour spoke, calling her attention and everyone else's back to him. "My mistress has taken him into her embrace. She calls him to his former self. She dictates the manner of his form. Now, let us see if he was strong enough to do her bidding."

His hands caressed the console, then took a sudden, strong hold of the control paddles. The candle bearers gave a different kind of gasp. He eased the controls forward. Again, the teleporter sparkled, but this time, it was the steady, familiar pattern of teleportation. When it ended, J.R. ,slightly younger and less buff, stood on the pad.

"What the..?" He started, then his knees buckled.

"Jimmy Ray!" Bobby dashed toward him, closely followed by the doctor. Both reared back when they got within smelling distance of his breath.

Dour said to his subordinate. "Present to him...The Mint."

Werl stepped forward, holding a pillow on which was a silver-wrapped candy. He knelt before J.R. and handed up the pillow, keeping his head ducked both in respect to the reborn and to minimize exposure to his exhales.

"Uh, thank you?" J.R. took the mint, unwrapped it with shaking hands and popped it into his mouth. He returned the wrapper to the pillow. He winced at the potent minty coolness.

"Bobby, where are we? Why's it so dark in here, and why are BiBi and GiGi holding candles?"

Bobby laughed. "Come on, brother. We've got a lot of explaining."

Together, he and Dr. Pasteur helped him up. He staggered slightly, but they held him steady as they led him to Sickbay, Bobby explaining about the ship. As they passed by Captain Tiberius, Jeb gave a small shake of his head. Better to get J.R. to Sickbay and checked out before a lot of introductions were made.

Instead, he went to his teleporter chief, who was now running a diagnostic. "Damn fine work, Dour."

Dour peered at him through hooded brows. "I do not know yet the consequences of this ceremony. There are many reasons it is not done, and only a few concern the victim."

"We'll cross that bridge when we get to it. For now, we'll make this room off-limits until you give the All-Clear. In the meantime, why don't you enjoy yourself?" He glanced from one candle bearer to the other, then back to Dour.

Dour, however, barely looked up. "My mistress needs me now. Go, you are free." He raised one hand to wave a dismissal.

The blonde whispered, "I would stay and learn at your feet, Master," but the other blew out her candle and pulled off the robe, leaving both on the floor.

"Well, you have fun, BiBi. I'll see y'all later." She sauntered out of the room, then picked up the pace until she caught up with Enigo, who with Loreli and Gel, were trailing behind J.R. and his escort, just in case.

"Hey, handsome," she said as she got close to Enigo. "I take it you're in charge of security? So, you wouldn't have really shot J.R., would you?"

"To save the human race? You bet I would, and sleep well that night, too."

"That's hardcore. I'm GiGi." She made to slip her arm through his, but Loreli pushed her hand away and skillfully slid between them.

"He recently experienced trauma to his side," she explained smoothly, but not smoothly enough that Enigo didn't falter in surprise.

"Uh, yeah, and I gotta work, anyway. Loreli, you okay escorting GiGi to the teleporter room so she can get back to the party? Gel and I got this."

Loreli slid her hand through the woman's arm and led her to a side corridor. GiGi hesitated and scowled, but true to Loreli's talent and training, they were chatting like new friends before they turned the corner.

Enigo and Gel continued following the others to Sickbay.

"What was that about?" Gel asked.

Enigo shrugged, then regretted it. Loreli was right; his side did still hurt, but he didn't think that had been her actual concern.

* * *

J.R. checked out and was released with a prescription for laxatives and a cortical monitor just in case any megalomaniac or psychic manifestations returned. Captain Tiberius released everyone to go to the party, but Loreli asked to remain and have herself checked out. Lt. LaFuentes, too, bowed out.

"I just want to go to my quarters, take my shirt off and put a cold compress on my new tatt," he said.

Once alone in Sickbay, Loreli explained the unusual thoughts and feelings she had been having since they had arrived at the planet. Dr. Pasteur listened, then had her lay on the table. He ran the scanners over her body while he took some clippings for analysis. Then, he set her under a sunlamp and mister to relax while he ran the analyses.

"Well, it's as I thought," he said to her half an hour later. "There's nothing wrong with you. All your genetic tests show standard for a Botanical. Your equivalent of adrenalin was a little high, but nothing unexpected considering what we've been through."

"But my reactions. If I had observed them in another woman, I'd have thought I was, well, jealous."

"I'm your doctor. Whatever you tell me is confidential. Are you sure you weren't?"

"Why would I be?"

He shrugged. "I want you to take tomorrow off. Spend some time in your pot. I'll let the Bridge know. You can go."

Obediently, she hopped off the table, smoothed the fronds that simulated her hair and started to the door.

He called out, "Oh, hey would you do me a favor? Would you take this analgesic to Lieutenant LaFuentes?"

* * *

Loreli gasped in surprise when the door to Enigo's quarters opened and the buff security officer answered, shirtless and in loose shorts. Yet, she didn't think it was in reaction to the red and slightly swelled area that marked his tattoo. Her sudden inhalation had sounded disturbingly similar to the ones she'd heard from several of the Lone Star women the past day. *What is wrong with me?*

She shoved the thought aside. "I'm sorry to disturb you, Enigo. Doctor Pasteur asked me to deliver this." She held out the analgesic.

He didn't take it but looked steadily into her eyes. She'd never noticed how deep and brown they were, like rich soil.

"Come in here and talk to me, Fronds." He turned back into his room, and she followed.

He motioned for her to sit on the chair and sat on the table. "What's going on, Loreli? You've been acting weird."

She almost wilted with relief. "So, you noticed, too? The doctor said there's nothing wrong with me, but..."

"You got feelings for me?"

Her words cut off with a laugh, but not at the absurdity of the idea. Rather, it was his straightforward way of asking. He was like that—spoke his mind, took charge. She—and everyone on the ship—knew where they stood with him. She'd always liked that about him. But did she *like* that about him?

Did she have feelings for him?

She started to avert her eyes, but they fell on the tattoo, which, given his musculature, was forming the most beautiful Fibonacci pattern. She brought them quickly to his face. "I...don't know how to answer that. I've never had feelings for anyone before—not feelings-feelings. I... Why are we having this conversation? I'm the ship's sexy. There are rules." And yet, she looked into his eyes and felt her blood swirling in complex spirals.

He nodded. "And there are ways around those rules, Fronds. You know it, and so do I. I looked them up."

"Why?"

"Answer me first: You got feelings for me?"

She found herself nodding. "I think so." The admission made her giddy. She giggled, then excused herself. "I feel like one of Ellie's romance stories."

"Yeah, well, Doall's too intuitive for her own good sometimes."

Loreli thought back to the Clichan mission and how she'd made Enigo play Loreli's jealous suitor. "You don't mean..."

"Yeah, I know it's cliché, but this isn't just lust or friends-with-bennies feelings. I know those feelings. This...is something more."

"Love?" She felt as if she were basking in a double sun and caught in a windstorm all at the same time.

His steady gaze broke into a smile and a chuckle. "Yeah, *amor*. Is that too strange?"

She found that she had been leaning toward him as if he were the suns. Now, she willed herself to sit back. "I'm not sure. I'm not human.

I'm not even meat-based. I'm not sure if, physically..."

He leaned toward her and kissed her. His lips were soft and his caress gentle, but while pleasant, when he leaned away, she had to admit that the experience was merely interesting.

Instead of pulling away in disappointment, he pressed his cheek against hers. "Oh, I'm not that easily discouraged. How about this?"

Gently, he blew on her hair.

Her fronds splayed open and a tingle spread across her body from the ends of her hair to the tips of her roots. When he stopped, she realized her eyes were closed and she felt a little dizzy. It was a very pleasant sensation, and she told him so.

"So, shall we start the paperwork?"

"Tomorrow," she said. "What fun is cliché if you don't have a little illicit romance?"

She blew on his hair and kissed him.

* * *

Aboard the Lone Star, the party was in full swing. Jeb had gotten to meet all his second cousins and third cousins and a plethora of cousins-many-times-removed. Definitely the biggest reunion he'd ever attended, but his mom would try to outdo it, he was sure.

Now, though, he was familied-out. J.R. had gone to bed, to sleep, he'd insisted, though Sue Ellen accompanied him. He hoped she remembered the doctor's orders.

The dancing had calmed to slow waltzes, and now to tired, half-drunk people swaying as they hung to each other. Most of the command crew had retired, and Jeb was ready as well. He made his way to where his cousin Bobby stood, staring out the viewport into a dark and anomaly-less sky.

Bobby sighed. "We changed their world, Jeb. We strode in, thinking about our own needs, and upset the balance of their lives. And now, we can't help them. They're dying, and so young."

Jeb set a hand on his shoulder as he, too, stared outward. "Live fast; die young. There was a time when being on a starship almost always meant you'd be killed by thirty-five. But people signed up, again and again—and here we are. Steely-eyed spacemen, the lot of us. It's really not the length of a life, but the quality with which it's lived. They're entering an Age of Heroes. I can't find it in my heart to pity them for that."

He left then, giving his cousin time to contemplate his words and the future of his ship and the people in it. Jeb had his own spaceship, chock full of steely-eyed spacemen, living their own Age of Heroes.

Amock Time

We open our story with the Impulsive orbiting an alien planet that looks remarkably earthlike in ways that make it easy for reader imaginations and special effects budgeting should this blog ever become a fully produced web series. After the theme song plays, we move into the ship, where Smythe, Doall, Cruz and most of the second-string bridge crew are watching the viewscreen. The whole Security Department and botanist Lieutenant Misha Rosien are crowded onto the bridge as well, and as we zero in on the viewscreen, we see why.

A squad of soon-to-graduate HuFleet officers, looking sharp in their dress uniforms, was marching across a grassy parade field on a sunny day (yellow sun, green grass... Just ignore the fact that it could be a football field when not being used as an outdoor stage for a science fiction show.) Oozing along in the right-front spot was none other than Gel O'Tin, the Impulsive's gelatinous security minion.

The squads halted and did sharp right-faces toward the grandstand where there sat representatives from HuFleet and civilian dignitaries—mostly local politicians, but one gelatinous being was plopped in between the bored mayor and the uncomfortable local who had been hired to sing the HuFleet Song.

As the candidates take their positions and listen to the Commander of Students make his speech, let us move forward now to the planet itself where Captain Jebediah Tiberius, Ship's Sexy Loreli, and Chief of Security Enigo LaFuentes sit on uncomfortable bleachers. (Alien bleachers, honest.) Enigo was smiling so hard, he even outshone Loreli.

Jeb leaned toward him. "All right, Lieutenant, you can say, 'I told you so.'"

Enigo shook his head. "Nah, you may have had doubts, Captain, but you supported me and stood by him all the way. But that guy..." He paused to point at the Globbal dignitary attempting to keep a shape that would not impinge on the mayor's manspreading or the singer's crossed high heels. "Him and all his planet deserve a piece of my mind."

"Success is its own revenge," Loreli reminded Enigo. He grunted and fell silent as the graduates were called forward.

Gel oozed onto the stage. The Admiral hesitated, unsure exactly how to pin ranks on a being with no uniform and a blob for a body.

Before the silence would turn to snickers, Gel puffed himself up and took the form of a human torso with strong, wide shoulders and a slim waist. The crowd roared approval as the admiral placed the rank on his now firm shoulders.

After the ceremony, they waited patiently as Gel and his classmates traded congratulations and goodbyes. Most would be heading off to new commands and new adventures. Gel would return to the Impulsive to take his place as Second Assistant Chief of Security. Everyone wanted his assignment; after all, redshirts survived on the Impulsive. Besides, Gel's a beloved main character; where else would he go?

Loreli pointed, "Look."

The Globbal dignitary had left the grandstand and made his way to Gel. His classmates traded some last words and left them to talk. The uneducated observer would think they were simply sitting there, quivering, but someone with Loreli's training—and by the magic of reader osmosis, you—could easily see that Gel was tense, even angry, but as the other spoke in their native tongue, he relaxed. They ended the conversation with a traditional, formal farewell. The moist slapping of their pseudopods could be heard across the field.

Gel hurried to his Captain and shipmates as fast as propriety allowed. He pulled himself back into the same buff triangle that had accepted his ranks. "Captain! Lieutenant. Loreli. I'm glad you could make it."

"Well done, Ensign," Captain Tiberius said. "Class honors. You do the Impulsive proud."

"Thank you, sir!" Gel quivered with happiness, and the captain couldn't help but feel the same.

From behind Gel, toward the podium, the Admiral was talking to the Globbal dignitary. He turned and pointed to Jeb, then summoned him over with a crook of his finger. The captain excused himself.

Enigo let Loreli offer her congratulations next, then said, "So, Ensign, you ready to take your new duties?"

"The ship is family! Beer me, sir!"

"Bueno. You get the mid-shift bridge duty."

"But I already have the mid shift."

Enigo grinned. "Yeah, but now when there's an emergency, you can handle it without waking me up. I might even get eight hours' sleep." He winked at Loreli. "But not tonight. We got the party of parties waiting for you on the Impulsive."

"Heck, yeah!"

Loreli said, "If you'd like to go ahead, I'll wait for the captain. I wonder what they're discussing."

They all turned to look at the trio, who seemed to be speaking amiably.

"I hope he's telling him what shit your people are for the way they treated you," Enigo said.

"Enigo," Loreli reproved. "They sent a representative all this way just to watch Gel graduate."

"Yeah, yeah. Success is revenge."

Gel shrugged. "Even so, there are some people on Plobloglup I wouldn't mind seeing just so I can rub their phagosomes in my success. But he was all right about it. Lots of 'fine representative of our people and our species potential,' and all that politicrap. If you'll pardon my Klatchian."

"I don't know what a phagosome is," Enigo admitted.

"Kind of like a stomach/liver/immune system thing," Gel said, "But we since don't have noses, I gotta rub something of theirs in my awesomeness."

"Trudat. Speaking of, my liver needs a workout. Loreli, sure you're okay waiting alone?"

Loreli laughed. "I don't think there are any dangers warranting a security officer to protect me, let alone two. Go. Enjoy. I'll drop by later."

Ten minutes and two propositions by local dignitaries later, the captain returned. He looked resigned.

"Captain?" Loreli asked.

He sighed. "We've been wrangled into freighter duty."

* * *

Captain's Personal Log, Intergalactic Date 676906.45

We're on course to Plobloglup to deliver sensitive scientific equipment and medical supplies. Da'ooze, the representative to Ensign O'Tin's OTS graduation, said it was a stroke of luck that the Impulsive was there. At maximum warp, our ship can get to Plobloglup twice as fast as the freighter that had brought him. We offered to give him a lift, but he insisted on staying a few extra days and returning with the freighter.

I have to admit, it all sounds a little suspicious to me. Ensign O'Tin has expressed doubts as well. I'm afraid he might not be adjusting to officerhood as well as we'd hoped. He's irritable, and not just from the hangover after his party. We also found him in the cargo hold, trying to ooze into the supplies. They were hermetically sealed, so no harm done, but his explanation for his actions seems downright paranoid. He believes Koos industries "has it in for him," and the medical run is a ruse to get him to his home planet. He refused to provide supporting evidence, however.

I've decided to let him remain on the ship instead of coming down to the planet, but I am concerned that won't be enough.

Ellie poked at her food to give herself time to think. Across the table, Gel sat, quivering and impatient as he waited for her answer.

"I don't know, Gel. I mean, you already got into trouble for trying to see what was in those crates."

"I know, but I was going to break the seal. You can use scanning equipment. Come on—one ensign to another, please?"

"What's got you so suspicious? You don't think we're carrying contraband, do you? HuFleet would never let that happen. Besides, we've never had problems with Plobloglup."

"Look!" he said loudly and rose to tower over her. Heads turned their way, and he returned to his normal shape. He started again. "Look, I have a hunch, okay? And it's important. But the LT and the captain don't believe me. What good is it to have rank if no one listens to you?"

Ellie frowned. How many times on the Mary Sue did she think just that? Maybe Gel needed someone to believe in him once more. "I'll see what I can do. But no promises. I need to find an excuse to go down there."

He said nothing, but she saw him gripping the table. "Are you all right? Your color is off."

"I'm fine," he snapped, as much as a globous creature can snap. "Please, Ellie, do what you can. I, I can't..."

"Can't what?"

He sighed. "Never mind. Just check."

He oozed out of the mess hall more slowly than usual. Ellie watched him go, wondering if she should say something encouraging. Then she glanced at the table.

Gel had dented the thick metal with his grip.

"Whoa," Misha Rosien said. She took the seat beside Ellie and stared at the damage. She leaned toward her friend, speaking quietly. "I didn't know Gel could do that."

"I'm not sure he realized he did," Ellie said. Her voice was equally hushed.

"Is he okay? He looks kind of...teal."

"He's freaking out about something, but he won't tell anyone what."

"I heard he got into trouble messing with some cargo. You don't think he got into something illicit at OTS?"

"Drugs?" Ellie would have laughed, the idea was so preposterous, but her mind was whirling ahead with possibilities. "Not Gel. Besides, why would he ask me to scan the containers, then? No, something is going on, but he's unwilling or afraid to tell the captain or Enigo the whole story."

"Maybe he's afraid they'll strip his rank? He was so proud to get into the officer training program. He wouldn't tell you?" Misha rubbed the nearest impression absently. It wasn't the first time someone had dented a mess hall table.

"No. He just asked me to trust him, but I'm not sure he trusts me. Which is silly. I mean, we're both ensigns." She knew she probably sounded self-pitying there, but why wouldn't he talk to her?

Misha snickered. "You're the Ops Officer—first-tier bridge crew. You're kind of a different breed. You know, I could talk to him."

"Would you?"

"Sure, why not? He and I kind of bonded when we were on shore leave at Rest Stop. And I'm nowhere near his chain of command. I'll give it a try."

"Okay, and I'll go scan those containers—just in case there really is something to worry about."

* * *

Ten minutes later, Loreli was walking alone through the corridors of the crew quarters. She was finishing her standard saunter around the ship and was weighing the relative merits of changing into tight, brightly colored workout gear and going to the gym or just calling it a night. As a Botanical, she kept her figure by careful pruning and didn't need to exercise, but a few yoga poses always improved ratings...

Looking at her scanner that told her there were twelve people in the gym.

Lost in thought, she was entirely unprepared for the doors in front of her to open and Lieutenant Rosien to come spilling out.

Misha reached up to her. "Loreli! Help me!"

A teal pseudopod stretched from Gel's quarters and pulled her back in.

The door shut on Misha's scream.

Loreli dropped her scanner and ran.

* * *

Captain's Log, Intergalactic Date 676906.75

Something is definitely wrong with our newest officer. Breaking into the cargo hold was one thing. Damaging furniture—it's been done. But Ensign Gel O'Tin has attacked a fellow officer.

"And so I called Security, ran for the nearest weapons locker, and stunned them. Twice." Loreli concluded her report to the captain. On the Sickbay bed, Lieutenant Rosien sat, a cold pack to her head. She hadn't said much. Loreli sat beside her, rubbing her back.

Jeb spoke gently, "You all right, Misha?"

She gave a small, miserable shrug. "It was all kind of surreal. I don't think he was trying to hurt me, but he didn't seem in control of his actions. I tried to run, but his reach! And then when he oozed over me…" She shivered and hugged herself, but nonetheless looked to the back room where Gel lay unconscious. "Captain, there's something wrong with him. He's a weird shade of teal. Are we even sure it is him?"

Jeb patted her arm. "Just rest a spell, Lieutenant. The doctor will check him out. We'll get to the bottom of this."

She nodded and leaned against Loreli. He went to the back room, which was separated from the rest of Sickbay by a force field. He wondered whether the measure wasn't a little extreme, then shrugged. He trusted his Chief of Security's instincts. Lt. LaFuentes lowered the field long enough to let him in. He noticed Enigo wasn't carrying a raser, but he knew that wasn't a sign of trust. In these close quarters and with Gel's reach and skill, if the Globbal wanted to, he could disarm his boss and stun them all before they could react. Enigo was instead trusting the ship's security systems to stun everyone in the room if their newest ensign got threatening.

Gel didn't look especially terrifying. In fact, he didn't look like much of anything. His viscous, semifluid form was contained by a large vat, the same used to hold nutritional soil for Loreli.

Instead of the stillness of unconsciousness, the fluid rumbled slightly, so that his surface rippled. He was, indeed, teal.

"Doctor?"

"I can't explain it," Dr. Pasteur said. "There is definitely something happening, but so few Globbals live outside the Plobloglup system, much less HuFleet, that the medical records are sparse. I do know this. He is undergoing some kind of phase change."

"Meaning?"

The doctor paused, trying with the author to find the best way to explain. "We don't normally see it, but Gel, like all life forms, has separate parts devoted to different functions—thinking, feeling, moving, digesting. Rather than physical organs, however, the divisions are mostly chemical. Still, they act separately, just like our feet don't generate testosterone, right?"

Enigo glanced at his boots doubtfully. "OK. So?"

"Well, all of his barriers are broken. His whole body is swimming with testosterone. And oxytocin and vasopressin... the Globbal equivalents, of course..."

Jeb, who grew up on the farm and had done breeding projects in 4H, said, "Hold up. Are you telling me our ensign is in heat?"

"This is beyond anything I've ever seen in a solid life form. Even worse, I'm not sure it's a naturally occurring phenomenon."

Taking what could best be described as a cake spatula, the doctor sliced into Gel's semi-solid form and folded a piece back. Under the thick teal layer, a blue spot lay like a bruise, with spidery threads branching out from it.

"What is that?"

"The source. It's artificial, but other than that, I can't tell you anything about it. I removed the nanites, but the damage is done."

Suddenly, Gel's form jerked away, splashing up against the other side of the vat. It returned to an even keel as Gel moaned. "What happened? I feel like someone shot me."

"They did," the doctor replied with his usual mildness. "Do you remember why?"

Gel started to bubble and mutter. "She knew this would happen. She planned it. That *blook*!"

The last word sounded more like a tar-like bubble popping, and the universal translator politely declined to translate it. He still hadn't tried to assume his usual form.

The three humans exchanged glances. "Ensign," Jeb said, an edgy drawl in his voice seldom heard by his crew, "if you're about to imply that Lieutenant Rosien 'asked for it...'"

"Rosie?" Gel froze. "What about Rosie?"

He started to tremble, sending tight fast ripples over his surface.

Doctor Pasteur set his hand on the edge of the vat. "Now, take it easy."

"What about Rosie?"

"If you don't calm down, I'll need to sedate you," the doctor warned.

"*Tell me!*"

"You went creepy ooze monster on her," Enigo said.

The doctor rolled his eyes.

Gel started to lap against the vat in his agitation. "Lock me away, Captain! I don't wish to be seen. No Globbal can explain. I can't be trusted right now. Maybe never again. Oh, Rosie, I'm sorry!"

Pasteur said again, "Gel, calm down."

"What's this all about, Ensign Gel?" Jeb asked.

"Or better yet, pour me into a torpedo and shoot me out of this system. Or into the sun—I don't care. Just don't make me go through with this. Please, Captain."

"Ensign Gel, slow down and explain it to us."

"I can't, Captain. It's too weird, and I don't want to be a creepy ooze monster!"

"Ensign!" Enigo barked, and he thrust his fist toward the vat. "Feel my steel!"

With reflex instilled over a year of training, Gel extended a pseudopod and wrapped it around Enigo's arm, hand to elbow. "I feel your steel." His voice trembled like his skin.

Enigo spoke with calm and strength. "Together, we are strong."

"Together we overcome."

"I feel your steel. Now, Ensign, are you ready? The captain needs a sitrep."

"Yes, sir… I don't know where to begin."

"Let's start with whatever is causing the blue spot. Is it some kind of…recreational drug?"

"What? No! It's… I'm going to die. Can't I just go die quietly somewhere?"

Enigo said, "You move out of that vat, and this room will stun us all. Now stop whining like a babimann and explain."

Gel pulled himself in, like a tide receding before a tsunami, but after a moment, he relaxed into a calmer state.

"I've been subpoenaed."

Jeb opened his mouth to say...something...but all that came out was, "Come again?"

"That 'representative' at my graduation? Just an excuse to slip me a subpoena."

The doctor snapped his fingers. "Of course! The nanite. It's a chemical summoner designed to activate a kind of homing instinct."

"Right," Gel said calmer and more miserable. "And the 'medical supplies'—if there are any— are just an excuse to have you personally deliver me so she can heap on even more humiliation."

Enigo, clearly as confused as his captain, said, "What did you do that your government would covertly inject you with some device that would make you return home or die of...horniness?"

The doctor winced. "Captain, perhaps, it might be better if I discuss this privately with my patient?"

Gel raised a pseudopod to indicate it was okay. He still had not assumed his normal form. "It's what I didn't do. They're summoning me to mate."

"You didn't take care of that before you left?" Enigo crossed his arms. While the others were surprised by this revelation, it didn't seem especially unusual to him. On the UGS Hood, all healthy and fertile inhabitants had to produce at least one offspring before being allowed to leave the ship. Enigo himself had three children, two of which were already looking for someone to give them a child so they could leave the ship, too.

Gel seemed to sink in on himself as agitation gave way to depression. "They didn't want me. I'm a Random."

(At this point, the author briefly considered bringing Loreli into the conversation, so as xenologist, she could give a quick explanation about what this means. However, it would add extra complexity and embarrass the heck out of poor Gel, so let's just keep his mortification among the guys for now, shall we?)

Dr. Pasteur said a soft, "oh" of understanding, then explained. "Gel's people are able to reproduce asexually via mitosis, but of course, that only works for so long in complex life forms. The Genetics Oversight Council strictly controls breeding when it comes to…comingling. Randoms are the offspring of those who defy this rule. But I don't understand. Your genetics are fine—better than fine in some cases."

"I was born from the Free Love movement. I wish I had been inferior. Then they would not have paired me with Vis Koos."

"That's whose crates we're hauling. That's why you wanted to look into them. You think she set you up?" Jeb said.

"She made my life on Plobloglup a living hell, Captain. She took every accomplishment I ever did and twisted it until it looked like a favor or a fluke. Finally, I wanted to be subpar, so she couldn't find a way to ruin everything I did. She wasn't the only one, either. I joined HuFleet to get away from her—from all my people. I was content to live among humans, just oozing by, doing the minimum to keep out of trouble. And that was fine—as long as I was a loser, the Genetics Oversight Council could assure themselves I was not worthy of mixing.

"But the LT found me and had me transferred, and no one here would let me stay a loser. I got ambitious. And I thought, I could be an officer."

"And now that you succeeded, you've proven you have worthy genetic potential," Jeb concluded.

Once again, Gel started to bubble and roil. "I was so stupid! Koos doesn't care. She's not going to take me. Now I have to go home, and she's going to humiliate me like she always did, only it'll be worse. It'll be in front of the Council and all of you and…"

"That's enough, Ensign!" Jeb ordered, and Gel fell silent. That is to say, he stopped talking, but he still blurped and burbled with agitation. "If you think some childhood bully is going to sway our opinion of you, you'd better have another think coming."

"Don't make me go, sir. Maybe the doctor could, I don't know, extract some DNA and send it to them?"

Enigo was grinding his teeth. "Captain, permission to speak to my ensign alone?"

Jeb raised a brow. "Will I regret it?"

"No, but she will."

The captain's eyes narrowed. "We will not be harming a Union citizen, no matter how much of a...blook she may be."

Enigo looked genuinely shocked. "What? No. She's gonna be the mother of Gel's kids, sir. No, way."

"No, she's not!"

"As you were, Ensign!" Enigo snapped at the tub of goo that was his subordinate. "No one under my command shirks his procreative duty to his species, *comprende*?"

Taking Gel's sullen silence as an answer, Enigo leaned against the edge of the vat. "You said you wanted to rub some phagosomes in your awesomeness. Time to make it happen. We start from the beginning. Tell me everything about this ceremony and how this blook is twisting it to make you look bad. We're going to make this right, you got that? Together. The ship is family."

"And family takes care of its own." Gel said. His voice sounded calmer than it had in days.

Enigo turned to look at the captain. "Don't worry, sir. Gel will make the Impulsive proud."

Which was just what Jeb liked to hear, though he never imagined it in this context. He nodded. "Keep me informed, Lieutenant."

As soon they'd left the field, Lieutenant Rosien pushed away from Loreli and straightened her uniform. "Sir, how's Gel—Ensign O'Tin?"

"He'll be fine once we get him to his home planet, but right now, he's very ill. He's truly sorry about what he did to you. You were right. He's not in his right mind. He doesn't remember any of what happened."

She nodded.

Jeb led the doctor to the far side of Sickbay. "You can't do anything about whatever is 'juicing' him?"

"If I could, I would have already, Captain. He fought off a double stun in record time, and he's not even complaining of a headache. The counteragents I introduced were absorbed like a placebo, and that scene that you just witnessed is him on the heaviest sedatives that I can safely administer and then some."

"How long can he stay like this?"

"Three, maybe four days, but I want to keep him here."

Jeb glanced toward Rosien. "No argument there. Captain to Bridge. Commander Smythe, how long until we reach Plobloglup?"

"A day and a half at current speed."

"Yeah, I think we can slow it down a bit. Why don't we go to Warp Two for now, give the engines a break."

"As you wish, sir." The First Officer gave the command to slow down.

"And I'd like to have someone check out those medical supplies headed to Koos Industries."

Ellie's voice interrupted. "Sir? Ensign Doall, sir. I'm in Cargo Bay Three, and..."

"Not vital medical supplies?"

"Some medical supplies? But mostly food coloring and gak."

"Gak?"

"Slime made with borax and glue, sir. Blues and teals. Shall I submit a report to HuFleet Command?"

"Prepare our report, but let's hold onto it for a spell."

At that point, Enigo stepped out of the force field. "Oi, Loreli? Can you come here? We need your expertise."

She cocked a brow in a way that was professionally skeptical and visually enticing. If there were cameras on her, they would have moved in for a close up. "Indeed? As a xenologist?"

"Yeah, that, too. Come on. This is going to take some work."

He realized then how everyone was gaping at him. "What? Someone's gotta coach him through the ceremony."

* * *

Captain's Log, Intergalactic Date 676907.75

We're doing our best to stall our arrival on Plobloglup, but a Koos Industries representative has contacted the Union and HuFleet to protest our delay. At Lieutenant LaFuentes' request, I've held off presenting our evidence of fraud, as he believes we need the element of surprise to make their plan work.

Unfortunately, if seems that no matter how good the plan is, our new ensign may not be able to pull it off.

Jeb met with the doctor, Enigo, and Loreli in the small conference room just outside Sickbay while Gel slept. His three officers looked like they could use some sleep, themselves. Enigo and Loreli leaned elbows on the table, frustrated and despondent, not something he usually saw in his officers. Could it really be that bad?

"This blook really got under his membrane, sir," Enigo said. "He's completely convinced that no matter what he does, she'll find a way to come out ahead. As long as he believes that, he's going to hesitate, and that's going to give her the opening she needs."

"I thought this was a mating. You make it sound like war," Jeb said.

"It is war, sir, and she has the high ground."

Loreli cut in. "The prejudice against Randoms is widespread and notorious. The Genetics Oversight Council selects mates using a blind DNA matching, so they don't know at the time whether a Globbal is Random or not, but the council itself does nothing to defeat the stereotype. Thus, even those that are genetically acceptable face so much stigma that they seldom reach their potential."

"Which then promotes the stereotype," Jeb said.

"Even worse, in a species which prizes the ability to adapt and overcome, Randoms take their failure as proof that their DNA is not desirable, after all. It's ironic, really."

"Yes, it is," the captain said. "Gel has adapted to human environments and living conditions. He's faced more challenges in his day-to-day life than most of his species will deal with in a lifetime."

Loreli nodded. "True, Captain, and we are trying to convince him of that. But that was not the irony I was speaking of. I… Well, see for yourself."

She pulled up a screen in the center of the table. Rotated before them was the cover with a desert background and a two-petaled flower— one pale green, one blue—in the foreground. The title said, "Random Encounter." She pressed a button and another cover appeared, this one with the same flower against a cityscape and the title "Random Affair."

"There is an entire genre of romantic and erotic literature devoted to mixing with

Randoms. There are even a few holovids, though they are not made publicly available."

Enigo leaned forward intently. He tapped one of the images—this one with the flower against a background of a meteor storm illuminated by the setting sun and entitled *50 Shades of Random* by Glu Fas—and opened it, flipping pages at, well, random. His brow knitted. "He swirled around me, then. I could not deny his nearness, how only thin membrane separated me from his coursing cytoplasm. My own cytol shivered in response," he read. "Dayum."

The doctor flicked an annoyed glance his way, then asked Loreli, "This is where you've gotten your material for coaching Gel?"

Loreli nodded without embarrassment. "To fit with Enigo's suggestions, I've pulled from the books where the Random is the romantic aggressor in the relationship. Unfortunately, Gel is utterly convinced he cannot seduce this Vis Koos, and any attempt to do so will only make him appear more foolish."

"Pulsie, pull up the profile data on Vis Koos," Enigo said, ignoring the conversation around him. Then he chuckled. "Loreli, did you read this one?"

Loreli glanced at the cover. "No, but I did scan it. It's not the best, literarily speaking, more equivalent to Random Encounter fanfic."

"This is the one we study," Enigo insisted.

Loreli hesitated. "Enigo. I think this is well beyond Gel's comfort zone. He doesn't think he can romance her, much less dominate her."

"Oh, he'll believe it, because it's exactly what she's secretly wishing for. Look." He pulled up her profile information and highlighted two pieces:

Favorite Color: Glu

Street she grew up on: Fas

* * *

Captain's Personal Log, Intergalactic Date 676909.50

The past two days, we've moseyed toward Plobloglup while we've worked out a plan that would satisfy the Genetics Oversight Council and restore Gel's reputation among his people. Discovering Vis Koos' secret hobby has given Gel new motivation, and he has thrown himself into preparing to meet her. Meanwhile, Enigo has had his security team investigating everything from her politics to her financial records. Now, it's time to zap down to the planet and see if all the hard work and study pays off.

Jeb waited with Loreli on the teleporter console. He tugged the collar of his dress uniform and readjusted the ladle and straw he wore on his belt. Even knowing why his Chief of Security had insisted on arming him this way, he felt silly. He rubbed his arm in an unconscious show of foreshadowing that should satisfy any creative writing majors reading the series.

Loreli gave him an amused glance. She wore her Surveillance Dress Uniform, the one for special ceremonies. It had sensitive recording equipment woven into the fabric. This allowed her to participate fully while getting a complete verbal and visual record of the proceedings. There had been talk of making the sophisticated fabric the standard for all away team uniforms, until those "on the ground" protested that some away missions were not worth reliving. Besides, cleaning them was a pain. However, in an unprecedented first (an admittedly redundant phrase), the GOC was allowing outsiders to witness the ceremony, and she didn't want to spoil the opportunity by rudely taking notes.

The doors to the teleporter room slid open, and two columns of six security officers each marched in. They halted smartly, faced each other and snapped to Honor Stance: Ramrod straight, heads high, the hands holding a raser pressed against their chests—the hands, not the rasers. This was an honor guard, not a suicide squad. Seriously, there's a whole 'nuther ceremony for that.

Next entered Enigo, looking every inch the HuFleet officer and warrior in his dress uniform. Somehow, the fact that he had a ladle and a straw strapped to his leg in place of a raser just made him seem even more badass. His metal straw gleamed, and he'd carved some notches into his ladle.

Next came Gel. His color had deepened from teal to blue, and he was obviously holding himself together by sheer force of will. Nonetheless, he wore his ensign rank, service ribbons, and medals, and he slithered to the teleporter pad with proud determination and took his place beside his commanding officer.

Doctor Pasteur brought up the rear, also in dress uniform but otherwise as bland as ever.

At Ensign Straus' command, the honor guard did a smart turn and faced the teleporter pad. "The ship is family!" they called out.

"I will make our family proud," Gel called out in return, his voice stronger than Jeb had expected. Ensign Straus had suggested the honor guard to send Gel off to his wedding in style, as a way to bolster his confidence. Looked like it worked.

Jeb nodded to the teleporter chief. "Zap us down." For once, Chief Dour did not preface his actions with any doom-filled intonations.

As they started to disassemble, Jeb caught Enigo scratching his arm. "Leave it alone," he muttered.

* * *

The humidity hit them as soon as they'd materialized enough skin to feel it. When their eyes formed, they took in dimly lit sky and a lush green land. Before them was a clearing of hard rock polished as smooth and shiny as Enigo's straw. To one side a round pool surrounded by flowers waited, empty.

Across from them stood a party of Globbals. One held a flower. Vis, Gel's childhood bully and future mate. On a pedestal were three officials of the Genetic Oversight Council. To their right awaited a half dozen others. Rivals. Gel had told them to expect that she might invite a challenger, maybe even someone he knew, just to humiliate him.

When they were fully materialized, the extra gravity made itself known, and they sunk slightly in the moist soil. Fortunately, HuFleet textiles were up to the task, and the special "starch" in their uniforms activated to help support the weight of their bodies.

Vis moved toward them, somehow managing to make the action of oozing look smug. "I see you brought your human friends. I wasn't sure you'd have the courage."

"And you have brought mine from my childhood. Couldn't find any friends of your own?"

She feigned innocence. "I'd have thought after so many years away and out of contact, you might welcome a few familiar faces. You always did seem to need some extra support. Shouldn't you Randoms stick together? They have, even though you fled. Are you sure you're up for this? You don't look well."

"That is because I burn." He made himself a little larger than her and moved just into her personal space. He spoke in a low, sultry tone. "And you know why."

No one would have guessed he'd spent hours practicing the move with Loreli and feeling like an idiot. When Vis hesitated, momentarily caught in his spell, he snatched her flower and swooped around her to the center grounds. There, he spread himself tall and thin, letting his medals and insignia drop dramatically to the dirt. "I respond to the summons of my people and the stirring of my cytoplasm. I offer my genetics to the next generation of our species. *Blurp-glop-gup!*"

With a showy corkscrew swirl, he went to toss the flower into the pool.

Vis tossed a clod of dirt in first. "*Blurp-glop-goop!*"

A triple sigh of exasperation came from the pedestal. Two servants hastened to clean the pool. Gel pulled himself into a rounded boulder of blue hate and rolled to the other side of the grounds.

"Shit. Here we go," Enigo muttered. The doctor took a subtle step back.

The centermost Globbal stepped forward. "Vis Koos, you have chosen Blurp-glop-goop, the challenge. Are you prepared to mix your genetics with the victor?"

"I am, if the victor is."

"Gel O'Tin, do you understand the choice that will be presented to you?"

"Just get on with it."

"Choose, Vis Koos."

She flattened herself in a kind of nod, then began to circle the arena, passing the platform first and moving counterclockwise. "As it has been since the dawn of days, when our forefathers left the ancestral pool, as it continues today..."

She passed the line of suitors.

"...and will continue through all tomorrows, I choose. This one."

She'd stopped in front of Enigo.

A collective cry of protest arose from her line of would-be suitors. Even the GOC representatives behind their spokesman looked disgusted. The spokesman said, "Koos, are you sure?"

"Has it not been said among the council that for our species to survive, we must introduce new elements? *I* will lead the way to a new generation of Globbals. I will sacrifice myself for the future of our kind."

Then she turned back to her human choice. "Unless, of course, you wish to refuse?" she purred—or rather, the universal translator analyzed the intonation of her pops and burbles and translated them into the nearest human equivalent, purring.

Enigo shrugged. "Nah. I'm willing to take one for the team."

"I...what?"

"Surprise," he cooed at her as he snagged the flower from her limp grasp. He pulled off his shirt and passed it with a flourish to Loreli—a completely unnecessary gesture, but what was a wedding without some drama? Hadn't Doall taught them that with the Clichans? Besides, it was wicked hot and humid. He did not understand the appeal of planets.

He stepped to the center and flung his arms high and wide as if he'd won a prize fight. His skin glistened. He hated sweating because of weather. But whatever. He knew he made it look good.

"I am Lieutenant Enigo Guillermo Ricardo Montoya Guiterrez LaFuentes of the UGS Hood, Chief of Security of the HuFleet ship Impulsive," he declared. "I am a Blood. A Warrior. A Lover— and a Father. I agree to father the generation of Koos de LaFuentes. *Blurp-glop-gup.*"

"No!" Gel roared. He threw himself like a wave at his commanding officer and swept him off his feet, then slammed him against the hard ground.

"Gel, stop!" Loreli cried out. She and the captain stepped forward. The two attendants who had cleaned the pool moved to block them from stopping the fight. Vis obligingly moved aside so they could have a good view.

Enigo thrashed at first, struggling to get his bearings as Gel held him in place and smacked him with gooey wave after gooey wave like

Satan's tide pool. The moist glopping sounds made low counterpoint to the human's cries. Finally, the chief of security grabbed the ladle from its strap. He scooped a piece of his subordinate and flung it way. It smacked wetly against the pedestal.

Gel screamed, but with rage or pain, no one could tell. He flung out a pseudopod to reabsorb the displaced blob, and Enigo used the distraction to get his feet under himself and try to jump out of Gel's gummy leg-lock.

The gravity and the sticky determination of his rival kept him pinned, however. He worked the ladle in earnest, flinging bits of Gel everywhere, using the flat of his hand to slap away any pseudopods that tried to disarm him. For a minute, it looked like a draw.

The Gel drew himself up and covered Enigo in a thick layer of cytoplasm. Enigo fought to keep his face uncovered with no luck.

Again, he struggled, but Gel held fast.

Enigo reached down and grabbed the straw. He put it to his mouth and blew out hard. Bits of Gel spattered away, but as soon as he took a breath, Gel had covered the hole again, and the second time, he was even faster.

"Ensign, you've made your point!" Captain Tiberius hollered from where they were still blocked by the attendants. "You can stop now!"

But Gel held his commanding officer in his enveloping grip. After a minute, Enigo fell limp.

The spokesman cried out, *"Blurp-glop-burble!"*

Gel lowered Enigo to the ground and oozed back.

The guards allowed the doctor to run to the human's side. He ran his scanner over Enigo and shook his head. "He's dead, Jeb."

Gel said nothing, but his body began to quake.

Jeb swore. "Take him to the ship. Loreli?"

She swallowed hard. "I'll stay, Captain."

As the teleporter beam disassembled the two into a gajillion pieces, Gel rolled to the captain.

"Are you ready to return to the ship, Ensign?"

"I'll stay," Gel said, his voice hard.

"Of course he'll stay," Vis added. "No one here will hold him responsible. He killed in ritual combat. The Union can't extradite him."

She turned her attention to Gel. "Of course, you'd have to give up your commission. No HuFleet here. But at least here, we'd understand it was a terrible accident."

"You misunderstand me," he snarled. "Nothing about this was an accident, and we both know it. I've killed my commander and my best friend, but you arranged for it to happen."

There was a gasp from the council, although none of Gel's old friends seemed surprised. The spokesman said, "Gel O'Tin. Explain yourself."

"Yes," Vis said, pulling herself up proudly. "Explain yourself."

"Gladly. And then, I will have my satisfaction."

He circled her slowly, not close enough to menace, but enough to keep her off-balance and paying attention. He spoke loudly enough for all to hear. "From the time you heard I was studying for my commission, you've been planning for this day. You sponsored the special interest group that fed the suggestion to the Genetics Oversight Council that we should add alien DNA to improve the gene line. Then you waited for me to succeed in a way the council could not ignore. Knowing that they would subpoena me at my graduation, you arranged to add a hormone manipulator so I wouldn't be in any position to refuse, and that I'd be so pumped I'd want anybody—even you. Then, you arranged a fake mission of mercy to make sure my ship brought me here. You brought my childhood friends—all of them Randoms, all less successful than me—but you never intended to select one of them. They were decoys as well as another way to humiliate us all while making yourself look open-minded. You chose my commanding officer, a human, to mock me while looking like a hero."

"I didn't think he'd accept," she answered. "I mean, we're so different. He couldn't be..."

"Into that kind of kink? You underestimate humans. Even more, you didn't count on the kind of loyalty I can inspire. You underestimated *me*."

He swirled around her then, almost touching. From how often it showed up in Glu Fas's books, it was Vis's favorite fantasy move. From the way she turned just a tad of teal, it seemed to have the same effect on her as it did the heroines in the stories.

Nonetheless, she managed a haughty voice. "Well, you seem to have it all figured out."

"Almost." He lowered himself then, slowly, and sinuously assumed his normal form. "What I don't understand is why."

"Why, what?" Her voice had a breathless quality.

Again, he leaned in. "Why, after all these years, you are still obsessed with me."

She laughed, but it was less sure than it had been when they'd first entered the arena. "The hormones have muddled your thinking."

"You'd like me to think that." He moved even closer, forming a thin sheet that isolated them from everyone else. He whispered, "Except I read your book, Glu. I know your secrets."

Vis's color started to pulse, and her voice shook. "I don't know what you're talking about. You're right. I did plan this. I did all of this to avoid mixing with you and your inferior genes."

"Once again, you underestimate me." He swirled around her, this time in the form of a double helix. As he spoke, its pattern changed.

"Another thing you didn't count on, Vis. My genes aren't just adequate any longer. I've spent a decade among humans. I've adapted to their environments—the lower gravity, the brightness.

It doesn't even bother me anymore. I've been exposed to new ways of thinking, new strategies for survival. All that is stored now in my DNA. You see, Vis, in your efforts to prove me inferior, you made me a superior specimen—and now, you're going to help me add that superiority to the gene pool. It was the last order my LT gave me. I may have killed him, but I'll never disobey him."

He formed enough of a face to look at Jeb. "Captain, I need half an hour, and then I'll turn myself in."

Jeb shrugged. "Take your time, Ensign."

"You. Me. Pool. Now. *Blurp-glop-gup!*" Again taking the form of a wave, he swooped up Vis and carried her into the gene pool.

Jeb politely turned his head and stepped away to go examine some flowers.

Loreli set herself down on a convenient rock where her uniform could record the proceedings. All things considered, it was going to make a fascinating paper.

According to tradition, the members of the GOC and the attendants watched. The females exchanged wistful, envious glances, while the males took notes.

Gel and Vis ignored them all.

* * *

Captain's Log, Intergalactic Date 676909.95

Gel's 30 minutes turned into 65, but that gave us time to present the Plobloglup authorities our evidence of Koos' wrongdoings, including fraudulent employment of a HuFleet ship. They had a police detail waiting for her when she emerged from the pool. She was going to have a lot of explaining to do.

We had some explaining ourselves, but that would have to wait until we were back on the Impulsive and heading out of system.

Jeb, Loreli, and Gel rematerialized to find the teleporter room filled with Security. Gel was back to his normal shape and color, although pale with sadness and exhaustion.

Gel did the Globbal equivalent of gulping when he saw his armed teammates crowding the room. "Guys?"

"Kneel!" Ensign Straus ordered, but before Gel could figure out how to position his body, the entire security team had fallen to one knee, arms extended in salute and fealty.

"Feel our steel!" they shouted.

"I...what?" Gel burbled.

Without raising her head, Straus said, "You have defeated our warlord in fair combat. By tradition of the UGS Hood, you must now take his place. We are yours to command."

"The Ship is Family!" the team replied.

"But...I... What?"

Before he could sputter further, the doors slid open, and Enigo stepped into the room. "Oi! I said over my dead body!"

"LT?" Gel's words came out as a squeak, then he said joyfully, "Enigo!"

Gel slooped off the teleporter pad and spun himself around his commander in a hug.

"Whoa, man! Too soon. I've been slimed enough for a day."

Gel backed up. He looked his commanding officer up and down as if convincing himself that he was truly okay. "I thought I'd actually killed you."

"As if! Pasteur wasn't sure you'd be able to control yourself, juiced up as you were, and Loreli wasn't sure they'd accept my defeat. So he injected each of us guys with imposazine in a sensor capsule. It went off when my oxygen level got below a certain point. Put me in a near death state. Once he got me to the ship, he gave me a counteragent. I have the mother of all headaches.

"We didn't tell you so you could keep up your performance. But speaking of, you have been holding back in sparring practice. That ends today, *comprende*?"

The rest of security surrounded him then, laughing, patting his back, congratulating him, and asking for a blow-by-blow of the fight.

As they started filing out the door, Straus asked, "Never mind that. What about that blook Vis? How did it go with her?"

"Vis? She wants me to contact her again anytime I'm in-system."

"Whoa! And..?"

"Are you kidding? Just because I was that good doesn't mean she was."

The door shut on their hoots and catcalls.

* * *

Gel stood before the closed door of Lieutenant Rosien's quarters, holding a potted plant and trying to get ahold of his courage. He'd picked up the flower from the mating grounds, but standing in front of Misha's quarters, he felt like he'd left behind the confidence he'd found there. Somehow, thinking he'd killed his CO was easier to contemplate than what he'd done to her.

Just do it, he told himself, before someone comes by. He'd checked the sensors before coming to make sure no one was in the crew deck corridors, but he couldn't count on them staying empty for long.

He shot out a pseudopod and activated her chime.

She answered in her pajamas. "Oh! Gel. Um. Hi."

She looked from him to the hall to him, to the inside of her quarters and back to him.

"I won't ask to come in," he assured her.

"Oh, okay. Thanks. I appreciate it." She still stood just inside the door, her hand not far from the controls.

"I just wanted you to know how sorry I am about what I did. I didn't mean to go creepy ooze monster on you."

"I know. You were, like, drugged, only worse, the doctor said. But you're okay now? Everything went okay on the planet?"

"Yeah, yeah. It… I should have trusted the LT—Enigo—in the first place. It's kind of a long story. Maybe some other time I can explain." When she didn't reply, he held out the plant. "Anyway, this is for you. They're the ceremonial flowers that grow around the gene pool. They're not supposed to leave the mating grounds, so don't tell anyone."

"Oh, wow. Thanks." She took the proffered pot, careful not to touch him, then cradled it against her chest.

"Things are going to be awkward between us, aren't they?" he asked.

"It's not that I blame you. It's just…"

"Creepy ooze monster. I get it. I just wanted you to know I'm sorry and I value our friendship. When—if—you ever want to…"

She was looking at the floor.

"Completely up to you," he finished lamely.

"Thanks," she said. "I appreciate that. So, good night."

He lingered for a few minutes after, staring at her closed door.

The No Brainer

Captain's Personal Log, Intergalactic Date 676916.56

After three months, it's nice to be back on the Impulsive and in my office. I enjoyed my time on Earth seeing family and helping my kin from the Lone Star get acclimated to their new world. The Lone Star underwent retrofitting, bringing some of their systems up to Union standards, while Union engineers learned about some advances the crew of the Lone Star had discovered. After all, they spent 300 years in a different galaxy finding their way home. The crew will remain on Earth for a few more months, exchanging information with HuFleet before each crewman decides what they'd like to do in this brave new world they've returned to. I did have the honor of bringing my kin home to Texas. We had one heckuva family reunion, let me tell you.

The Impulsive was due for a tune-up herself, so it's been in dry dock getting upgrades on the drive systems and the replicators. Filedise apparently upgraded its software while we were dealing with the Paleos, and both the Union and HuFleet were given a great deal on the upgrades if they went in together, so we'll be cutting edge. Of course, "cutting edge," meant delays in installs as they worked out unexpected issues in compatibility. I think Deary reversed the polarity three times before it took, but he loves that stuff.

The crew, of course, took advantage of the long stretch of time off. Most scattered to the ends of the galaxy, visiting friends and family as I did, but others stayed closer to home. I was surprised to find Lieutenant LaFuentes volunteered to handle security during the upgrades. He usually trusted that to his second, but instead, he recommended Ensign Gel for some courses at the Academy. Well deserved, too, but Enigo could have passed the security detail to his third and gone home to The Hood like he normally does. I'd have thought the experience with the Lone Star would have made him a little homesick. After all, they were the same model generation ship. Loreli also chose to *remain and take an adjunct course at LunaTech on comparative reproductive biology.*

Of course, it didn't take long to find out why.

Loreli and LaFuentes? Well, she could do worse.

Captain Jebediah Tiberius paused his log to process his feelings. Yes, she could do worse, indeed. Enigo was a good man. He'd been surprised but amused to approve their request for a three-month secret romance waiver with option to escalate. Now, he was looking at their HuFleet Form 214-heart-exclamation-winky face: Request for three-month secret romance followed by big reveal. Things were going well for them, then.

Happy as he was for their budding romance, he couldn't help feeling a little bit of sadness. He had taken Loreli under his wing since he'd rescued her from that mad botanist's lab. Was it 10 years already? He'd seen her bloom into a responsible and exceptional member of his crew, and it gave him a real sense of paternal pride. Now, it felt like he was giving her away.

Which was theatrical, he knew. He wouldn't be walking her down the aisle yet. Or was it transplanting pots? What kind of wedding would they want?

As he was chuckling at his folly, his door chimed.

Chief Lawrence "Loggy" Loggins, quartermaster for the Impulsive, poked his head in. "Welcome back, Captain. How's the new chair?"

"It's great. The cup holder's a nice touch. What can I do for you?"

"Well..." He hedged as he took a seat on the opposite side of the desk. "I hate to bring this up, but... How's your toilet paper, sir?"

"Pardon?"

"It's just that some of the crew have been saying theirs is licking them."

Jeb snickered, but then he realized his quartermaster was serious. "Ooo-kay..."

Loggy grimaced. "At first, I thought the company was taking their revised 'Enjoy the Go' slogan too far, but I contacted the manufacturer, and they insist it's not their doing."

"Practical joker?"

"Maybe, but I've reloaded the replicator file twice, and each time, the resulting TP has been more...tactile...than meets most people's comfort levels. I talked to Lieutenant LaFuentes, and he's going to get his CompuSec people on it. In the meantime, I'd like your permission to take a shuttle to the supply warehouse and fill it up with as much TP as it can carry, just in case our joker is wily."

"You can put out an All-Hands notice, too. I don't mind a good joke—and it is kind of funny—but you gotta know when to let it go. Taking anyone with you?"

"Nah, the warehouse crew will help me load, and that way, I can pack it in the copilot section, too. We've got 285 people on this ship. We go through a lot of TP fast. I'll be back and have it stowed before we leave."

"Carry on, then."

The quartermaster nodded and made to leave. At the door, he turned back. "Sir? Have you noticed how happy and—I don't know—relaxed Lieutenant LaFuentes is? It's kind of eerie."

"Maybe he had a chance to unwind on the long leave."

"Maybe, but he spent it on the ship instead of going home."

"'Home' is the UGS Hood."

A light went on behind Loggy's eyes. "Yeah, that probably explains it."

* * *

"Captain on the bridge!" Ensign Ellie Doall's voice rang out.

Jeb raised a brow at Lieutenant LaFuentes, who answered with a shrug. As long as his Chief of Security had been sticking around the ship while it was in dry dock, he'd assigned him a different mystery: Figuring out how their Operations Officer inevitably knew when her captain set foot on the bridge, no matter where she was facing or where he entered from. Some mysteries were meant simply to be appreciated, it seemed.

The rest of the crew were at their stations. Doall, of course, stood at the Ops, her hands flying over the console, likely doing three things at once and all of them perfectly. She hadn't mentioned where she'd spent her vacation. Loreli stood beside her at the Xenology console. She really didn't need to be on the bridge right now, but as Ship's Sexy, it was her right and duty to be visibly present to inspire the crew. First Officer Phineas Smythe had trimmed his hair and mustache according to the latest styles of his homemoon, Calisto. Lieutenant Tonio Cruz cracked his knuckles over the helm. Jeb noticed the small medallion attached to the console— Saint Danika Wash. Cruz had been very proud that he and his nona had been invited to the Vatican for the canonization of the patron saint of starship pilots.

Since the rest of the main characters are not on the bridge, but elsewhere on the ship actually doing their jobs, we'll just sum up by saying the rest of the bridge staff were at their consoles, watching indicator lights, typing in commands, and in the case of the second-string crew in the bullpen, wistfully dreaming of the day when someone on the bridge suffers a debilitating accident and they could bravely dash forward to take their place.

"What's the word on the TP Prankster?" he asked Lt. LaFuentes as he made his way to the command chair.

"Nothing yet. This guy is good," LaFuentes replied, "but *non te preocupara*, sir. My team will keep at it until there's nothing left to go on."

Jeb hesitated at the stairs. Had his Chief of Security made a potty joke? Even Doall had paused in whatever it was she was doing to gape at LaFuentes, but he focused on his console as if he'd said nothing out of the ordinary. "Security has finished the last sweep of the ship. We're secure to launch."

Doall turned back to her console. "All stations report ready for launch, Captain."

"Activate dramatic running light sequence and let's get out of here."

Sadly, I don't have a dramatic exit sequence for you, so please imagine the scene in *Star Trek: the Motion Picture* when the Enterprise leaves drydock. I'll wait.

...

Ready?

"We've cleared space dock," Cruz said as the last of the fanfare died down and the normal sounds of ship operations could once again be heard. "Course is set for the Pack Nebula."

"Cool. Let's go blow up a brown dwarf!"

* * *

Captains Log, Intergalactic Date 676918.70

The Impulsive is en route to the Pack Nebula, home of a dozen-plus Wolfe-Rayet stars. We'll join our sister-ship, the science vessel, HMB Inconceivable, which will be conducting an experiment in stellar manipulation. Our primary job is to lend a hand—and maybe a tractor beam—if the Inconceivable gets into trouble. The Logics ship Rational Plausibility is joining us to observe.

Commander Angus Deary is with the Inconceivable to assist in some of the preparations. He's an engineer, not a scientist, of course, but the designer of the hardware, Commander Grant Jardin, was his long-time lab partner at the University of Strathclyde in Glasgow. They reunited during the upgrades to the ships, and he was invited to advise on a particular problem that was baffling their scientific crew. When I asked him if he was able to solve the issue, he laughed and said it was a "no-brainer." I feel like there's a joke in there, but he's not been willing to share just yet.

And speaking of jokes, our practical joker continues to elude our security department's investigations. It has become something of a game for them, but others of the crew are growing less amused.

One of the bullpen crew shrieked when Loreli stepped onto the bridge.

The ship's sexy stood at the lazivator, her usual calm, alluring demeanor slightly ruffled, and with good reason. Her normally fern-green skin was pastel pink.

"What happened?" Ensign Doall asked.

"It would seem our practical joker had reprogrammed my evening nitrate supplements." Despite the calm in her voice, the narrow-eyed glare she gave to Lieutenant LaFuentes said how pissed she really was.

"Are you okay?" he asked with uncharacteristic gentleness.

She swept past him and took her place at her station beside Doall. "Doctor Pasteur and Chief

Botanist Chen say there's no harm. The process is similar to changing the color of orchids. It's not permanent."

Doall nodded. "Oh, like changing your hair color—Captain on the Bridge!"

Half a heartbeat later, the lazivator doors finished opening, and Captain Tiberius stepped out, accompanied by his First Officer, Commander Smythe. Both stopped abruptly when they saw the pink vision at the Xenology console.

The captain cleared his throat. "I got the report from Sickbay, Loreli. Are you feeling all right?"

She gave him a warmer smile than she had to Enigo. "Quite fine, Captain, thank you. As Ellie was just saying, it's not dissimilar to changing the color of one's hair. I just wish it had been my decision."

"Have you found our joker yet?" the captain asked Lt. LaFuentes.

"No, sir. We're not finding any traces of tampering at all, and yet... This guy is good."

"Well, playtime is over. Helm, how long until we're at the Pack Nebula?" he asked as he and Smythe took their seats.

"Two more minutes at this speed, then five at sublight—fifteen, if you want to take the scenic route," Lieutenant Tonio Cruz said from his station. On a spot above the controls, next to his St. Michael prayer card, he had a new photo of himself and his nona standing in front of a racing shuttle. He'd told everyone earlier about how he and his nona had taken her shuttle on a scenic trip around Italy. Apparently, he, too, was still in a vacation frame of mind.

"The straight route, please. We're expected." Jeb said, then he opened a shipwide channel from his seat.

"Attention, all hands. This is the captain. In six minutes, we'll be at the Pack Nebula to help the science vessel, the HMB Inconceivable, conduct a highly volatile experiment—one that, if anything goes wrong, just might destroy both our ships and maybe this sector. It's time to focus, which means the replicator shenanigans stop now.

"We're coming into a complex and dangerous mission after a long break, but I expect everyone to operate at their top efficiency. You are the best crew in HuFleet, in no small part to your innovation and creativity. However, let's apply that to the problems at hand. Captain out."

"Slowing to sublight," Cruz said, and the inertial dampers obligingly provided a physical cue of a slow jerk to signify the change from warp to impulse drive. Meanwhile, the screensaver changed from the streaks of light to a colorful nebula full of pulsating stars. Even though it was a computer simulation where colors were assigned to certain frequencies outside the human visible spectrum, it was nonetheless a beautiful sight. Everyone paused to enjoy the view.

Everyone except Loreli, that is. She was looking at the message on her console. "*Eres muy bonita en rosa.*" She glanced to the side to see Enigo give her a quick wink.

The Pack Nebula, of course, was not nearly as pretty as the viewscreens showed, at least not to human eyes. Wolf-Rayet stars burn blue and are best known for their lack of hydrogen, which astronomers believe was blown away by stellar winds. Thus, their hot helium cores are exposed, but since they are aging supergiants, they're not embarrassed by it.

Normally, a nebula features one supergiant star, but in this case, there were fourteen Wolf-Rayet stars; hence, the name "Pack Nebula." The astronomer in the author's mind who so-named the nebula was exceedingly pleased with himself for this moniker and went further by naming the stars "Alpha Male," "Alpha Female," "Beta Male," etc. His one regret was that normally, after Alpha, Beta and Omega, people didn't get the reference.

Nestled in the far corner of the nebula, the HuFleet ship Inconceivable and the Logic science ship, Rational Plausibility, orbited Gamma Female. "Nestled" may seem a relative term, given the comparative size of the ships vs. the incredibly huge distances between stars, and yet depending on the speed in which you traverse the distance, things are a lot closer than you think. Especially when your helmsman is a hotshot pilot who was raised by a feisty Italian grandma who at 110 was the oldest person ever to win the Solar 500. As the Impulsive threaded a solar flare, more than one officer in the bullpen wished the captain had chosen the "scenic route."

"Hey, flyboy!" the computer of the Impulsive barked. "I just had a full-body buffing. Don't singe my hull."

"Okay, okay, *guastafesta*," Cruz muttered.

"*Chifa il grande*," the Impulsive retorted.

Captain Tiberius exchanged glances with his first officer. They'd been told that the Impulsive had been upgraded with enhanced initiative subroutines, but they hadn't realized all the implications.

From Ops, Doall said, "We're in communications range of the Inconceivable."

Glad for the distraction, Jeb ordered her to hail them. The replay of the close call was switched to the bridge of the Inconceivable, where Commander Deary stood next to Captain Cary Vizzini. Vizzini was a small man with a round face, a high voice and an air about him that, even through the translight transmission, projected, "I love my job." Deary, tall, thin and black, was a stark contrast, especially since he was scowling.

"Oi, Cruz. I just had that ship buffed," the Chief Engineer scolded.

"So I've been told," Cruz said.

Captain Vizzini said, "Welcome to our playground, Captain."

Jeb stood and stepped forward. He didn't need to, of course, but the cameras would take the cue and close on him, forestalling any further arguments between his two officers. "Glad to be here, Captain Vizzini. How goes the preparations?"

"Thanks to the assistance of your very skilled and most creative chief engineer, we are on schedule and ready to go. The Logic team is double-checking our equipment and math."

"Our science team has looked your calculations over as well," Jeb said. "They didn't understand all of it, but they're very excited."

"They did find where we forgot to carry the one, which resulted in an increased chance of punching a hole into a mirror universe where we'll encounter our evil doppelgangers," Vizzini said, wagging a finger at him and grinning.

"Which is why they're excited."

"Us, too! So, would you like to come aboard and see our work?"

"I'm sure some of my science and engineering teams would like to—Ensign Doall, as well—but I was a history major."

"What if I said our ship was in imminent danger and you needed to come aboard with your senior staff?" Vizzini wheedled, and both captains laughed.

"But then Ensign Doall would have to stay here to command the ship. That's hardly fair. How about after the tour, you, your science team, and your senior officers come to the Impulsive for a pre-experiment celebration? Might not get a chance if we create a black hole, after all."

"Yeah, that would really suck," Vizzini said.

On that lame, yet popular, pun, they made arrangements and Doall left to join the science team in the teleporter room.

When the door closed, Jeb said, "Well, we have some time to kill. Enigo, Loreli, since I am a history major, I'd like to hear more about what you've learned about the Paleos. Join me in my ready room?"

The couple kept professional demeanors as they followed the captain, but inside, their hearts were light. They knew the update was an excuse. Captain was going to interview them for their three-month secret romance renewal.

* * *

Loreli walked into her quarters singing to herself in the language of her people, which was more of a swaying of the thick aloe-like leaves that served as her hair and a motion of the skin that made sounds that only the most sensitive ears picked up. Despite the morning's prank, the shift had gone surprisingly well. Everyone seemed to approve of her new coloring, and once she got over the disconcerting surprise at seeing her own skin a totally different part of the spectrum, she actually enjoyed the change. Like Ellie said, it was not dissimilar to a human dying her hair.

It offered new opportunities as well. As ship's sexy, she was not limited to standard HuFleet uniforms. She has several styles and colors to choose from, ranging from gray to pastel green. Most, however, clashed with her natural colors, so while she had a few alternatives for specific occasions, she seldom wore them.

She decided her nails needed to be a different color, as well; while their current blue matched her uniform and had gone well with her normal shade of green, it was too bold against the pastel pink. She wanted something more suitable for the party.

I have an hour. I can try several colors. Perhaps pearl, she thought, though a stem green might be nice, especially if I'm to be Enigo's *orquidea*.

She felt a thrill move over her at the thought, and she paused at her nail station to close her eyes and indulge in her happiness. After discussing with the captain, they'd agreed on a 3-month extension to their secret romance contract; if things did not work out, they could cancel out quietly; otherwise, they'd apply for public reveal.

She felt a warmth blow across her hair just as hands slipped over her waist.

"Enigo!" She spun into his embrace. When she could at last pull herself from his kiss, she said, "How did you get in here? What if someone saw you?"

"You kidding? No one was going to see the way I came." He jerked his thumb over his shoulder to where the grate to the ventilation ducts was ajar.

"You learned how to get to my quarters through the air vent?"

"I'm Chief of Security. I know how to get anywhere on this ship through Jeffries tubes or air vents—and so do my people. I keep telling the captain you should all know it in case Pulsie gets invaded, but he says there's too much potential for invasion of privacy."

"I can understand that."

"*No te preocupara*. Pulsie would alert you—and Security—if anyone was using them to be a peeping tom. I mean, unless his sensors are down, in which case, we're probably invaded, which is the point."

"So why didn't Pulsie alert me?"

"Secret romance clause! Besides, this is part of my culture. On the Hood, it's the height of courtship for the guy to crawl through the vents of enemy territory—or the overbearing mom—to see his woman."

"I offered to play the overbearing parent," Pulsie said, "but Lieutenant Loverboy didn't think it was necessary."

"Hey, Pulsie? Go run a diagnostic or something." When the ship did not reply, he took Loreli's hand and led her to the couch. "I figured we had a little time before the party."

Tempting as the couch was, she wouldn't let romance interfere with her duties. "I have to do my nails first."

"I can work with that," he teased.

She set the nail station to pale green gel and enjoyed the sensation on her fingertips while Enigo stood behind her, breathing into her hair. That was a sensation to be enjoyed as well.

* * *

As expected when any two HuFleet ships have a get-together, the party was raucous yet within protocol. The Inconceivable won the coin toss and chose a lively soundtrack of Logic/Human mashups. Jeb was not a fan of Logic music, having had to endure a painful semester at the Academy with a roommate who insisted on it for studying, but he had to admit "Standard Variations on

Kol'nar's Theory of Quantum Shearing" actually worked quite well on bagpipes.

One of the security team was discussing the replicator prank with the Logic First Officer. Jeb wondered at the large crowd that had gathered. The mystery was solved when the unwary Logic asked if they had discovered the perpetrator, and his officer replied with a completely straight face that no, and they had nothing to go on.

Jeb sauntered past, feigning obliviousness to the Logic's confusion as the conversation deteriorated into a series of puns and one-liners, and joined another group. This, too, included a discomfited Logic, but at least it was a true discussion about their mission.

The small group focused on the Logic and Captain Vizzini, who spoke with animated motions of his hands. He reminded Jeb of his own helm officer, and he decided if the two ever got into a discussion together, they'd have to warn everyone to give them a wide berth lest they get smacked by an arm waved while emphasizing a point. Vizzini paused in his monologue to introduce Jeb to the Inconceivable officers as well as the Logic, Lieutenant Fle'ek.

Doall was with the group, listening intently and trying hard to look at the attractive Logic science officer while not looking like she was trying to look at the attractive Logic science officer. Fortunately, everyone was so enthralled in their captain's conversation—and socially oblivious in general—that no one else noticed.

"Of course, we don't know what's going to happen," Captain Vizzini continued after they had exchanged greetings. "I mean, if we knew, it wouldn't be science, now would it?"

"I do not understand. What else would it be?" Fle'ek asked.

"Engineering, of course!"

"But the experiment itself does not make sense," Fle'ek persisted. "We did verify the mathematics and the equipment, but it's the underlying theory that continues to perplex us."

"Oh, we've got more than a theory. We've got three!"

"Yes," Fle'ek responded with the patience his people were famous for but without the insufferable arrogance shared by most of his species. "One: The warp cores will fuel thread-level weaving processes, thus rebuilding the hydrogen layer and transforming the star from Class W to Class G or K. Two: The warp cores will overbalance the energy level, causing the star to collapse into a black hole, potentially taking your ships and ours with it. Three: The resulting explosion will cause a rip in the space-time continuum, dragging us into a mirror universe where we will all have to pose as evil representatives of ourselves until we can steal the technology we need to recreate the failed experiment and send ourselves back. To be completely honest, I am unsure how anyone came up with such a speculation in that level of detail."

"Well, you know how theories are," Vizzini bluffed. All members of HuFleet knew about the mirror universe but were strictly prohibited from telling any other species about it. Not only was it potentially dangerous for other species to know how the evil human empire had enslaved all the other sentient races in its known universe, but their fashion sense was just embarrassing.

Fle'ek replied, "It would seem that, when it comes to the human use of the term 'theory,' I do not."

"Well, you're on the right mission to learn, then." Jeb said, with a wink at his peer.

"Yes, you're definitely on the right mission to learn about the genius of human scientific questing," Vizzini enthused, and around him, the Inconceivable scientists nodded vigorously.

"I do not see how," Fle'ek deadpanned, and Ellie choked daintily on her drink.

Captain Vizzini gave him an almost fatherly—which is to say, patronizing—smile. "Let's walk you through this, shall we? How many cockamamie experiments has the human race performed?"

After asking the ship to define "cockamamie," the Logic science officer immediately replied, "Since the first contact between our two species, five hundred and ninety-seven, counting only those experiments that were conducted with our knowledge."

"And how many led to findings that changed the course of science?"

"Two. First, the attempt to unlock telekinetic abilities in humans led to the emergence of neurothread theory and the discovery of midichlorians."

Doall sighed, "Too bad midichlorian threads were linked to narcissism and bad judgment. Telepathy would be so tactically useful."

Fle'ek nodded in acknowledgment and continued, "Second, the tesseract distilling process, which results in biofuels that burn at 302 percent efficiency and inspired the field of tesserchemistry."

"Oi!" Lt. Commander Deary protested. "Don't be forgetting the 90-degree polarity reversal."

The Logic gave him a small bow. "I had not. Large-scale applications have not yet been found."

"Ach, 'tis a handy little trick, though, isn't it Jardin?" Deary asked as he swigged back a thimble-sized drink that nonetheless seemed to kick him like a mule. After all, the tesseract distilling process didn't just make potent biofuels.

"There's more than that," Doall chimed in. "Sheb Wooly-Mendelson's attempts to prove that the unicorns of Magihapi had in fact been violet instead of pink changed everything we knew about the evolution of the creatures on that planet."

Fle'ek raised an eyebrow in strong protest. "His attempt to unlock the color gene caused a mutation that resulted in monocular vision and carnivorous appetites."

"And flying. We had no idea they were apex predators. Well, until they ate Mendelson and his team, but it changed our understanding of life on that planet."

"It sparked an accelerated devolution of the entire ecosystem. It was a spectacular failure."

"But we were the first species to prove that accelerated devolution was even possible," Ellie countered, and the science officer of the Rational Plausibility had to pause in his argument. Jeb hid his smile behind his drink. All those lunchtimes she spent arguing with Lieutenant LaFuentes were starting to pay off.

The Inconceivable's captain chimed into the silence. "Exactly my point! Failure is simply advancement in a different direction. So, are you learning anything?"

"Yes," Fle'ek replied slowly. "The human capacity for rationalization is unfathomable."

They all had to drink to that.

At this point, Captain Tiberius decided it was time to change the subject. "So, philosophy aside, how exactly will this experiment go? Not to influence the results, but how can we be sure we aren't sucked into a black hole?"

"That'll be a no-brainer," Grant said as he grabbed a bottle of ItsGreen and refilled his glass and Commander Deary's.

At the table itself, Chef had just set out the main course of the evening—a turkraken, a hideous yet oddly tasty mix of a turkey and a squid. Enigo was explaining the concept to Loreli as she eyed the food dubiously.

The Impulsive's chief engineer grinned back and then explained. "Novatic Operational Beta Ray Adaptive Interferometry Nucleosynthesis Regulator. NO-BRAINR."

"I...am not sure those words belong together," the Logic science officer Fle'ek said, and Jeb had to agree with him.

Deary tried to explain, but Doall asserted that he was simply stringing unrelated words together again.

Deary replied, "Och, that's how it goes with acronyms. Suffice it to say, without that handy little device to apply adaptive interferometry for measuring the nucleosyntheses, we could be in big trouble before anything's registered on our sensors. But dinna you worry. We've got everything under control."

At that moment, there were shouts as the turkraken suddenly gathered its tentacles and launched itself straight at Enigo. Before the chief of security could react, it had wrapped itself around his face. Loreli grabbed it by the roasted wings and pulled, but it freed one tentacle to slap her, and she fell back. Ensign Gel O'Tin whipped out a tentacle of his own and caught her before she fell into the Ridelian sweet puffs.

One of the Inconceivable officers dashed in to make a second attempt to free Enigo from the culinary fright and was also slapped away. He crashed into the espresso bar. He screamed as hot steam seared his arms and hands.

Four members of security pulled out their rasers and stunned both the culinary creature and their superior officer. Enigo dropped unconscious to the ground, and the turkraken, still in possession of whatever counted for consciousness in a main course, started to scurry away, only to be phased until it stopped, shook, and exploded.

There was silence and the smell of roasted meat.

Doall called Sickbay.

"Another result of 'science'?" The Logic First Officer asked as he peeled a singed tentacle off his cheek.

"Baking is science; cooking is art," Doall said as she presented him a bowl to drop his piece into. "Even so, with your permission, Captain, I'll get this to the science lab so we can figure out what's going on. This doesn't normally happen with food," she added to Fle'ek.

"Indeed. May I join you?"

The two gathered some pieces and exited together, talking animatedly.

Meanwhile, Sickbay personnel had arrived and were putting Enigo and the Inconceivable officer on stretchers while one lucky tech examined the sucker-shaped bruises on Loreli's otherwise perfect cheek. As they exited, a trio of janbots snuck in the open door.

"Good job, everyone," Gel said to the security team. "The Boss is going to be so proud of you all."

(Of course, you know Enigo will be. If you don't remember—or know—why, check out "A Day in the Life" in *Space Traipse: Hold My Beer, Season 1.*)

* * *

Loreli waltzed into Sickbay with her usual beautiful-and-caring-but-unattainable demeanor, but really, she was fighting the butterflies fluttering in her trunk. Her secret romance with Enigo had been relatively easy when the ship was mostly empty but for a few crew and maintenance personnel. Now, surrounded by people who knew and loved her well, she found herself wondering if she and Enigo were giving themselves away with every chance look. It did add an element of excitement. She'd have to rely on her training, lest she give her emotions away.

"Loreli!" Trevor, the medtech who had helped her, smiled with mild infatuation. That often happened after physical contact. "Are you feeling all right? How's your face?"

She gave him her friendly, enigmatic "Mona Lisa" smile. She'd spent hours with the holographic interactive model of the original painting, stepping into the display and contorting her features until she got it perfectly. "Thanks to your expert ministrations, I'm fine, thank you, Trevor. I came to hand-deliver the results of our analysis on the turkraken and check in on our patients."

"Hey, Fronds," Enigo groaned from where he lay on a diagnostic bed. He didn't bother to open his eyes and gave her only the weakest of waves. Despite herself, she grinned. Four raser blasts, even set on stun, would give even their valiant Chief of Security the mutherofal headaches.

On the bed next to him, the officer from the Inconceivable was upright and grimacing rather than wincing as the doctor ran a dermal regenerator over his scalded arms and reassured him that yes, he would be able to play the flutaphone again—if, of course, he knew how to play the flutaphone in the first place.

"It doesn't really matter," the young man replied. "It's the only one of its kind. The computer made up a whole new music style for it. If I miss a note, I can say it's just improvisation."

According to *The Ship Sexy Handbook*, Loreli should go greet the healthy crewman with polite familiarity en route to Enigo's bedside. This she did, but then hesitated as she approached her love. It wasn't the secret romance that made her pause, however. Normally in her role, she would lean toward Enigo solicitously, allowing him a brief glimpse of her cleavage, but considering he had the heels of his hands pressed against his eyeballs, she didn't think he would appreciate it.

Instead, she set her hand lightly on his shoulder. Squeezes were reserved for the unconscious, the critically ill, or those in a state of high agitation, so she resisted the urge, much as she'd come to enjoy the feel of his taut muscles.

"How are you feeling?" she asked.

"Violated," he groaned. "That thing didn't just grab my face, it frenched me halfway down my throat. Doc, you sure it didn't lay eggs in my stomach or anything?"

"I did a complete scan," Doctor Pasteur said. "There's nothing but traces of turkey grease and squid ink."

"No wonder I'm nauseated."

"That is probably more the effect of being stunned simultaneously by four of your security members."

"Yeah." Despite his pain, he had pride in his voice. "Best security team in the fleet. But you're sure...?"

"It wasn't alive," Loreli assured him. "We ran multiple tests. It was pure replicated meat. Somehow, the cells were programmed to react to being prodded."

"You sayin' it was a practical joke?"

"Apparently."

"When I find this guy, I'm buying him a beer— then I'm stunning him four times."

"You have a joker, too?" the Inconceivable officer asked.

Enigo removed one hand just enough to peer at his fellow patient. "You didn't hear about our toilet paper that licks?"

"That's...interesting. No, but we have one, too. My flutaphone? It was supposed to be a

French horn. Then I was replacing a wall speaker. It's a standard replacement file, but now, the replacement morphs into a talking fish whenever it's activated."

Doctor and medtech snickered, but Enigo asked, "Did you guys report it to HuFleet?"

"I don't know. I'm Maintenance. I doubt it. Everybody kind of likes Walleye."

Enigo sighed. "We thought this was some crewman with a warped sense of humor. LaFuentes to the captain, we got a problem—and it ain't just the main course."

* * *

Captains Tiberius and Vizzini entered Sickbay to find the doctor arguing with LaFuentes about giving him something more for his stun symptoms while Loreli stood nearby, being beautiful and supportive and, Jeb admitted to himself, doing a damn fine job of not showing how concerned she was over her boyfriend's condition.

"Imposazine is an exact science," Dr. Pasteur said. "You've had the maximum dose for stun symptoms."

"So what? What's the next dose good for?"

"Ironically enough, if you had actually been implanted with alien eggs, the next level dose would have dissolved them into an inert compound that would then pass harmlessly through your system."

Enigo paused to consider this. "Would it have helped my headache?"

"No. Now, lie down. Your headache and nausea will pass in a couple of hours—less, with your...resolve."

Jeb cleared his throat to get their attention. "Mind if we have a word with the lieutenant first, Doctor?"

"As long as he doesn't leave the bed."

Vizzini asked, "Where's my man, Sopren?"

"I cleared him. He's gone to warm up for the concert."

"Excellent. Well, Lieutenant, please explain what you meant when you said we've been sabotaged. I can assure you our preparations have been under the very tightest security."

"Yes, sir," Enigo said. Per with doctor's orders, he did not leave the bed, but even though it was set to an upright reclining position, he was sitting up and perched on the edge, an effort which was costing him. A normal human would still be unconscious after such a concentrated stun fire, but Enigo was Hood born and bred. He had an instinct to fight to consciousness even under the most extreme circumstances. This instinct which paid off in the many gang fights and skirmishes that were a normal part of life on the Hood, but for which he was paying with the migraine of a lifetime.

He swallowed, took a slow breath against the nausea, and explained. "Not the experiment, per se, sir. It's about the replicators. I heard you are having a problem with a practical joker? Us, too. I don't think we can chalk that up to coincidence."

"But they're harmless pranks," Vizzini protested.

"One tried to at once choke and smother me," Enigo pointed out.

From where he was mixing chemicals in a beaker, the doctor said, "He's not kidding. He had some impressive bruises on his neck."

"Whatever the intentions," Enigo continued, "the fact remains that both of our ships have been affected, and independently of each other.

Captain—Captains—I recommend all replicator activities be suspended except for mission-critical components, and that those be double-checked before being used. And we should definitely alert HuFleet and see if other ships have been affected. In the meantime, I'd like Ensign Sisco to coordinate with his counterpart on the Inconceivable to see if they can find any commonalities that will suggest how our ships came under the same attack."

"Sounds prudent to me. Vizzini?" Jeb nodded, and with the decision made, the doctor returned to Enigo's side, and insisted he lie down. Loreli moved in to help him ease back against the mattress, leaning forward just enough to allow everyone a peek at her perfectly sculpted cleavage. Jeb made a note of how well she was maintaining her duties as ship's sexy even while emotionally committed.

"I don't see how it's an attack," Vizzini said, after shaking off the momentary distraction. Being a science vessel and not a combat ship, the Inconceivable did not rate a ship's sexy. "Still, you know the old saying, 'Never get involved in a land war in Asia.' I'll alert my ship to suspend replicator operations. However, I think we can hold off introducing our two CompuSec officers for a couple of hours, don't you? Only, Lieutenant Rurr is part of the band, and they've been practicing this new set for a month now. Sopren's weird new instrument is something that has to be experienced to be believed. You might say the sound is...inconceivable."

Enigo winced, but then again, so did everyone else.

Dr. Pasteur cleared his throat. "If that's all, Captains, I think my patient should take his rest." He handed Enigo a glass with a cloudy liquid.

"What is it?" Enigo asked.

"Hangover cure—my great-great-great-grandfather's recipe. Not exactly meant for stun shots, but the symptoms are similar, so... Drink this down, then I'm going to give you a cold compress, and you're going to lie quietly with the lights low for at least four hours—one for each stun. If you sleep the night here, all the better for you. Is that understood?"

Enigo looked to his captain. Jeb nodded. "Ensign Straus can be in charge."

"Too bad. You'll miss the concert," Vizzini said. "Maybe we could pipe it in?"

"No," both doctor and patient said.

He sighed, "As you wish. Though perhaps Lieutenant Loreli...?"

"I'd be honored, Captain." Loreli finished smoothing a compress on Enigo's forehead and patted his shoulder. Then, she slipped her arm through Vizzini's and allowed him to escort her out. Jeb gave a nod to both Pasteur and Enigo before following.

* * *

Captain's Log, Intergalactic Date 676920.35.

Lieutenant LaFuentes' instincts were right on target as usual. As it turns out, HuFleet has been getting complaints about unusual replicator failures. Almost all of them ran along the same lines as those affecting our ships. There have been delays in reporting since, like us, most commanders thought them harmless pranks. Packing materials where the pillows were filled with helium instead of air, weight sets made of negative mass... It wasn't limited to ships, either. A dessert machine on the recreational station,

Hava Blast, produced enough crème brûlée to fill a room neck high. Vacationers thought it was an activity and dived in, literally as well as figuratively. The foodie reviews said it was the best dessert presentation ever until the machine produced a match.

Ensigns Sisco and Rurr and their teams, along with HuFleet Central, believe the problem to be with a corrupted replicator file that then, in turn, spread to corrupt existing files. Knowing this, they are now working to identify and weed out the corrupted code. They've also contacted Planet Filedise. The entire planet is devoted to a single purpose—designing, patenting and selling replicator designs for most of the known universe. The longest-operating business in human history, it prides itself on customer service; I'm sure they'll have a crack team rooting out the source on their end as well.

In the meantime, everything else is proceeding according to schedule. The Inconceivable is ready to launch its experiment. Commander Deary is back on the Impulsive and monitoring the *experiment and his NO-BRAINR from the bridge engineering console while Doall monitors the star itself from Ops.*

Incidentally, Doall left the concert early in the company of the Logic scientist Fle'ek. I might have suspected an interspecies liaison, except that all the Logics in attendance left halfway through the first song. Later, I found Doall in one of the briefing rooms with three of them, scowling over equations while they explained with their famous patience.

Jeb ended his log and stepped out of the briefing room onto the bridge. As usual, Doall called out his presence, though she stifled a yawn to do so.

"Late night cramming session?" he asked as he took his seat.

"And yet I still only understand half the math, sir," she lamented. She reached under her console for a lidded mug and took a sip from it.

"Well, fortunately, there's an entire ship of mad geniuses who can handle that this time. Cruz, are we in position?"

"Aye, Captain."

"Engineering?"

Deary replied, "Engines are optimal and NO-BRAINR is ready to engage."

Jeb went through the rest of the stations, each confirming their readiness to monitor a history-making event, to pull the Inconceivable from the edge of a newly made black hole or to do battle with their evil doppelgangers, whichever result actually manifested.

"All righty, Commander Smythe, put us on Yellow Alert. Impulsive to the Inconceivable and the Rational Plausibility. Vizzini, we are ready when you are."

On the viewscreen, the view split into three windows. One showed the bridge of the Logic ship: clean, efficient, quiet. Their captain gave a nod of acknowledgment. A second screen showed the star itself, innocently shining along, minding its own business, unaware of the violence about to be done to it in the name of science.

The third showed the bridge of the Inconceivable at a wide angle, displaying all its personnel, from the helmsman nervously poised to warp the ship out of danger to the third-redundant sensors tech playing Galaga.

Vizzini signed a datapad and handed it to the waiting yeoman and then clapped his hands together gleefully. "Excellent, Tiberius! The warp core should reach overload in about 15 seconds. We're ready to 'port it into the heart of the star in five...four...three...two...now!"

Of course, the teleporter was in a cargo-bay-sized lab on the other end of the ship, but they thoughtfully relayed the teleporter whine so everyone could feel the same excitement—and relief—that the lab team felt when they sent the ready-to-catastrophically-explode device off their nice safe ship and far away into the heart of a dying W-class star. The chief scientist reported the warp core's reintegration within the star, with its force field intact but being eaten away by the star's incredible energies. He rattled off some other technobabble that sounds terribly impressive on television but really just means {scifi-science, blah-blah, something big and explody is going to happen, blah-blah}. He ended his explanation just in time for the explosion.

At that cue, the viewscreen changed to the star itself. Nothing was seen of the warp core, but the entire star bulged, then returned to its usual size, as if containing the urge to belch.

"We're getting telemetry," the voice of the scientist said as the star slowly started to change. Below it, a ticker tape started to scroll numbers and reports from the other science stations on the Inconceivable, interspersed with the continuing odds from the pools of both ships. Deary was adding his own commentary at scheduled frequency, primarily consisting of "nominal," "nominal."

While the visuals weren't especially comprehensible, the tones of the scientists' voices grew increasingly confident. That is, until Ensign Doall said from Ops, "Captain…? I'm not sure those numbers look right."

Before Jeb could alert Vizzini, Deary cried out, "Och, jobby!" Similar exclamations of surprise came from the Inconceivable. Then, the screens went blank.

The Impulsive went on Red Alert.

It should be noted that the captain did not call for Red Alert. The AI of the Impulsive just decided to do it on its own. This was part of its new initiatives features. Captain Tiberius didn't like it. He was all for initiative, mind you, but he did not like being taken by surprise.

Nonetheless, he filed that away for later conversation with the ship programmers—preferably off ship—and reacted according to his training and protocol. "Cruz, get a tractor beam on the Inconceivable and get ready to move. Deary, what the hell happened?"

"I… I don't know. I've nae seen anything like this. It's like space-time is unraveling."

"How the…? Impulsive to Inconceivable, we are reading a thread unraveling, can you confirm?"

The popping of a champagne cork was their first reply, then the viewscreen showed the bridge personnel, all laughing and slapping each other's backs. A holographic marquis proudly declared, "Humans break physics again!"

The star's color was starting to wobble; Jeb looked at the time hack, did a rough calculation, and shivered. Given the speed of light and their distance, they were seeing a reaction from before the core was launched. On the bridge of the Rational Plausibility, the Logics were no longer so calm but were hurrying about. Their ship, too, was on alert. They were no longer sending audio, a fact the Logic captain was just coming to understand, it seemed, because he had leaned forward in his seat and was speaking intently. Jeb could not make out the words, but he did get the gist.

Broken Physics Bad.

"Vizzini!" Jeb shouted. "I've got a ship that thinks this is a red-alert situation. I need a threat assessment."

"We don't know yet," Vizzini answered as he accepted a glass of spumante from his yeoman. "The sensor data is unlike anything we've ever seen. Isn't it exciting?"

"Captain," Cruz interrupted, "I can't get a tractor beam lock. It keeps bouncing off their shields."

"Reverse the polarity," Deary said.

"I have! And 90 degrees, both ways. It's not working."

"Captain," Doall cut in, "the Rational Plausibility has engaged engines, but it is not moving."

"Cruz?" Jeb said. It was both question and command.

The helmsman's hands flew over his console. *"Santo Michele!* We're stuck."

"Hey!" Enigo said and pointed at the viewscreen. "I don't think stars are supposed to spark like that."

Indeed Gamma Female had not only started wobbling its colors but spitting out moon-sized fireballs. One headed straight for the Inconceivable.

"Brace for impact!" someone on the Inconceivable called out across the ship. People yelped and clutched desks, chairs or each other. Someone thoughtfully threw himself over the case of champagne.

The meteor passed through its shields as if they weren't there.

And then, it passed through the ship.

The last thing they saw on the viewscreen was Vizzini mouthing, "Inconceivable!" and then the viewscreen went to static.

"What the hell happened?" Jeb demanded.

Of course, when any ordinary human utters such a phrase, you might get commiserations of surprise, like, "Whoa! What was that?" or "I don't know. Weird!" When a starship captain makes such an exclamation, he expects a scientific answer—fast. A starship captain in HuFleet expects a practical answer. And Captain Jeb Tiberius?

He's expecting his crew to be doing something about whatever the hell "that" was.

"Trying to reestablish communications," the second ops officer reported.

"Analyzing the frequency of that...anomaly and matching shields to deflect," Lieutenant LaFuentes called from Security.

Ensign Doall, who was trying to determine the answer to the big question, huffed in frustration. "Sir, these reading don't make any sense."

Meanwhile, at the helm, Lieutenant Cruz was working the controls and alternately praying and cursing. "She won't budge, Captain."

First Officer Smythe said, "Captain, we're receiving injury reports from all over the ship. Falls, pulled muscles..."

"Were we hit?" Jeb turned back to his First Officer. He took a step—and his foot flew out from under him. He landed flat on the deck.

"Captain!" One of the second-string crewmen in the bullpen shouted and ran to his aid even as Smythe was telling her to stop.

She made three steps when suddenly, she toppled forward and landed on the captain, knocking the air out of them both. She tried to shove herself off, but her hand slipped and she flopped onto him again.

"Ensign," Jeb gasped. "Slowly."

She pulled herself on her elbows so she was nose-to-nose and chest-to-chest with the captain. She paused to make sure she had her balance, then gently sat up. "I'm so sorry. I don't know what happened. It was like my foot got stuck."

"Pulsie, what's the status of the inertial dampeners?" Jeb asked as he carefully stood, dusted himself off, and make his way slowly to his chair. He held up a hand to stop his First Officer before he could ask if he was all right.

"Inertial dampeners are working perfectly, Captain," the ship responded.

"It's true," Doall said. She had a scanner in her hand and had stepped slowly away from her console, moving with gentle, deliberate steps toward the scene of the fall. "The equipment is working according to specs—but inertia isn't."

* * *

Captain's Log, Intergalactic Date 676920.90

The failed experiment has resulted in pockets of variable inertia throughout the ship. We've been lucky so far; the crew has been mostly unharmed, suffering only pratfalls and accidentally tripping into a member of their preferred gender for an awkward and embarrassing interlude. Now that the crew is aware and moving more deliberately, the incidents have diminished in frequency, but still seem to happen most around our ship's sexy. Loreli is, of course, handling it like a professional, but it's getting distracting. I tried giving her a security escort, but when she and Lieutenant LaFuentes fell down a Jefferies tube together and were stuck for 45 minutes, I decided we'd all be better off with her doing research alone.

The one person seemingly unaffected by this is Minion Leroy Jenkins, who seems able to charge his way through any inertial nullity. Lieutenant LaFuentes does not seem surprised by this. He's assigned Minion Jenkins to patrol the ship, mapping the inertial null zones and moving people when they are stuck. We're hoping a map of the affected regions will help us deal with the problems and give us an understanding of what happened.

Whatever odd phenomenon has affected inertia is also to blame for our communications issues. The communications section and Ops have amplified our hand-held communicators, and by trial and error have found the best places on the ship in which to get a signal to the Rational Plausibility and the Inconceivable. All three ships are unable to contact our respective fleets or anyone outside of each other.

At least we haven't seen any new surprises. We're on Yellow Alert and Ensign Doall is coordinating the research of all three ships.

Ellie sighed and paced the floor, grateful that the captain had allowed her to retreat to a private office. She hated showing her frustrations in front of her crewmates, and this problem was the most frustrating she'd ever encountered.

On the viewscreens was the relayed image of the science team of the Inconceivable and the direct comms of Lieutenant Fle'ek. The science team were showing their own signs of stress; Fle'ek, of course, looked as placid as ever. Ellie admired that calm, especially in such a handsome face.

"I'm telling you, the math is wrong," Doall said yet again.

"You have said yourself that you understand perhaps half of the computations," Fle'ek countered. Somehow he did so without sounding insulting.

"Just because I don't understand the theory doesn't mean I can't tell when the math is wrong. It doesn't add up, figuratively speaking, I mean."

From the Inconceivable, Basil, the civilian scientist who was the advisor for the warp core/star experiment scoffed. "It is completely obvious what's happening. The math isn't wrong. It's changing. The universe is rewriting itself."

Ellie could almost hear the "I told you so" in his tone. She'd met him at the party and they'd immediately disliked each other. His abrupt, arrogant manner contrasted completely with the Logic's gentle neutrality; fortunately, that only made Doall more stubborn about asserting herself.

"Then why isn't it consistent? On our ship, people are falling into each other, but your ships don't have that problem. Plus, we've mapped the ship three times, and the pockets of inertia are never in the same place twice, nor are they following a pattern."

"That we can see. We need more data points," Fle'ek said.

"Yes! Exactly—but not about inertia. Or rather, not just about inertia. We need to know every anomaly on each ship. Something else is going on here that goes beyond the experiment."

"How could you possibly know that?" the scientist on the Inconceivable demanded, but one of the others at the table said, "Hang on." The rest of what he said was lost in static.

Ellie tried and failed to suppress a frustrated growl. "Doall to Reece. I'm losing the Inconceivable. Can you try stepping to the right?"

"Sure, but I'm hearing them just fine."

"As are we," Fle'ek cut in "Ensign Pang is saying ninety-eight percent of the experiments on their ship are working perfectly, and producing the exact results they expected. That is indeed anomalous. As their captain so eloquently stated, if everything happens according to one's expectation, it is not science."

But Doall's mind was processing other information. *Pang. I never met her.* "Basil, say something. Anything. It doesn't matter what."

"What? What kind of request is that?"

She could hear him perfectly, including that "You're an idiot and we're wasting time," tone she knew only too well from her training years on the HMB Mary Sue. "Thanks. Pang, now you."

Her confused reply was clearer than before but it nonetheless cut in and out, along with the visuals.

"Okay, thanks. Now, Fle'ek—can you have someone else take the comms—someone female that I don't know?"

He raised one eloquent eyebrow to show he, too, was not sure where she was going with this experiment but complied. She stepped into view and spoke, and the comms again started to spurt, but not as badly. When Fle'ek moved off-screen fully, the comms got worse.

"That's the missing math," she said. "We need every anomalous incident—and not just what, but *who* was affected, and their honest feelings about the effects of the incident."

"Their feelings," Basil stated in the exact tone Ellie expected, the one that used to make her retreat into a tiny shell of self-doubt, but now told her she was on the right track.

The rival, the love interest, and me.

Fle'ek, however, was already following her chain of logic. "The observer influences the observation. Which would explain why we are experiencing so few problems, except where we are in contact with you humans."

"Right. As Logics, you suspend your expectations or hopes in order to wait for the natural results to show themselves."

And, as she expected, Fle'ek took on a thoughtful, approving expression. She'd seen it several times over their short acquaintance—a slight pursing of the lips, a brightening of the eyes. She wondered if he knew how good he looked. She wondered if he realized how the expression gave her a warm, happy feeling.

Then their eyes met, and she knew that he did.

* * *

Several hours, much arguing, and many romcom-style incidents later, the science teams presented their findings to their captains. It was a three-way comms, still being relayed, but thanks to Doall's revelation, the lines were clear as long as she, Fle'ek, and Basil led the conversation. Or more to the point, as long as she led the conversation, with Basil and Fle'ek chiming in like two arbitrators, or the angel and devil on her shoulder. But that just reinforced her theory as well.

"It's nonsense. There is no way emotions can figure into an equation," Basil insisted after she presented her theory to the command crews of each ship. They had gathered in their respective briefing rooms. It should be noted that on the Impulsive, First Officer Smythe, having nothing to contribute to the scene, was in fact on the bridge doing his job and commanding the ship while his captain was otherwise occupied with the larger issues.

"You say it's nonsense, but the evidence supports my theory," Ellie responded. She felt gleeful, almost giddy inside. While on the HMB Mary Sue, the push-and-pull effects of having a nemesis and a mentor/potential love interest had forged her from a shy, brilliant cadet with low self-esteem into a brilliant and self-confident officer. Now the process was propelling her to new heights. "The laws of this new...pocket universe if you will, are far too localized around people.

"Let's start with the obvious. I analyzed the incidents of every time someone tripped into someone else. I then repeated the events in a controlled setting. Only people who were attracted to each other, openly or secretly, fell into each other, and only when they were within staggering or catching distance. And the stronger the attraction and the stronger the secret, the more likely the couple would bump into each other and stay stuck."

With her heightened awareness, Ellie noticed LaFuentes shifting uncomfortably in his chair. A glance at the viewscreen showed Loreli, safely absconded in her room, also felt sheepish. He and Loreli were the outliers in the equation both in frequency and duration, but she had a theory about that, too. "Lieutenant, I think I may be to blame for you and Loreli. Remember our encounter with the Clichans? I had 'shipped you and Loreli pretty aggressively to complete the mission. Somehow, that's been picked up by the threads of this new universe."

"But that was long before this mission," Commander Deary protested. On the Inconceivable, Basil threw up his hands in a "Yes, exactly!" motion.

"But it's still in people's minds—even LaFuentes' and Loreli's. Now, let's look at the experiments. There are 312 experiments running on all three ships. Three hundred and five have concluded, which is odd enough in itself, but even more so when you realize they all completely meet expectations of the lead scientist. The rest are either still running or met the expectations of the strongest-willed scientist on that team."

"What about this experiment?" Vizzini asked. "We had three potential conclusions, and none of them involved rewriting the laws of physics."

"I'm afraid that's not true—is it, Basil?"

"It was an offhand comment!" the lead scientist retorted.

However, Commander Deary's face grew ashen. "Bugger me," he whispered, then in a louder voice explained. "That little git was poking his nose into Grant's and my work while we were building the NO-BRAINR. He kept insisting we were doing it wrong and how we were going to end up rewriting the laws of physics instead of monitoring them. Are you telling me he was right?"

"So they did screw it up. That's not my fault!"

Doall shrugged at Basil, then spoke to her captain. "It is, and it isn't. I checked the records. Basil's exact words were, 'NO-BRAINR? What an appropriate name. It should be a no-brainer not to throw another variable into my carefully planned experiment. Adaptive Interferometry Nucleosynthesis Regulator. If your regulator ends up rewriting the laws of physics...' At that point, Commanders Deary and Jardin said—well, the exact words aren't important, but basically that it was impossible. And yet, later in the records, they laughed about both putting money in the

Inconceivable pool for the experiment to rewrite the laws of physics."

"As a joke," Deary protested. "We were yanking Basil's chain. There's no way our device could rewrite anything."

"We spent weeks on the design," Jardin added. "We ran every conceivable test—and a few Inconceivable ones. The design was perfect."

Doall nodded. "And then, you put the design specs into a replicator. The same replicators that are creating running shoes that run away from their owners and ear drops that make people's ears drop off."

Doall's revelation was met with thoughtful silence as everyone contemplated her words. Deary and Jardin cursed themselves for their folly while blaming Basil for putting the idea into their heads. LaFuentes was appalled that so dangerous a virus was still able to penetrate his HuFleet's systems. Captain Tiberius was rubbing his behind—because it still hurt from his fall, but if people thought he was praying, he was fine with that.

The humans were all wondering whose ear had fallen off while the Logics were hiding their grimaces of sympathy for their afflicted crewmate.

LaFuentes broke the silence. "So let's destroy the NO-BRAINR."

Before Ellie could protest, Basil said, "That's what I'm saying. And then we need to destroy that star. We're going to need another warp core."

"We are not giving you our warp core," the captain of the Rational Plausibility said.

Jeb added, "Don't look at us. But it seems to me if the NO-BRAINR is causing this, we should use the NO-BRAINR to stop it."

"We don't even know how it's programmed wrong," Deary protested. "We checked everything before it deployed, and it worked perfectly."

Ellie nodded. "That's the problem. It is working perfectly, just differently than expected—just like every other bizarre thing that's been replicated. So, it's not rewriting the laws of physics, but regulating a different set of laws."

"And in order to regulate them, it has to enforce them in our universe," Jeb concluded.

"Therefore, if we remove the enforcer, our universe will reassert itself?"

The captain of the Inconceivable spread his hands. "The universe does have a way of healing itself."

Jeb nodded. That explained why they didn't continue to encounter their mirror universe selves. He turned to Ellie.

The science teams had already discussed this and other alternatives and come to the same conclusion that LaFuentes had—blast the troublemaker into oblivion. Now, under the expectant stare of her captain and crewmates, she felt a trickle of doubt. Still, what alternative did they have?

"It's our best shot, sir," she said, "but I can't help but feel like it's too easy."

The captain nodded. "All right. Keep thinking about alternatives in case you're right. LaFuentes, prep the rasers. You'll have to compensate for the weird pockets of inertia outside the ship. Deary, Jardin: Can you replicate a second NO-BRAINR?"

"Aye," Deary answered. "But I dinna see how that wouldn't make the problem worse."

"Oh, we're not turning it on. I want you to replicate it, then take it apart and scan every inch. Get down to the thread level if you have to. Do the same with the TP and the running shoes and any other wonky thing. And get Sisco and Rurr to assist. Someone has tampered with our replication systems, and we need to get to the bottom of it."

Basil cleared his throat in a parody of politely interrupting. "Excuse me. Shouldn't we consider the problem at hand?"

"I am—and if Ensign Doall's instincts prove true, we'll need a Plan B, and that means we need to understand why things are acting the way they are, and how we can influence them."

As Ellie expected, Basil rolled his eyes and muttered something under his breath about her instincts, but she didn't let his sarcasm sting her. Instead, she basked in the faith her captain placed in her...and in the admiring and thoughtful gaze she believed she felt coming from Lt. Fle'ek.

Captain Tiberius paused at the entry to the bridge and watched as his command team retook their positions—in particular, the pretty little ensign who had already tripped into him twice. Now that he understood that whatever the device had done was affected by romantic attraction, he understood why she always seemed to have a little extra pink in her cheeks when she spoke to him, particularly when apologizing for crashing into him. It wasn't the first time he'd had to handle a crush by a junior officer, and he made a mental note to make sure she got put on an away mission. Odds were, she'd find a new love interest to make her forget her puppy love.

That, or she'd be horribly killed in the line of duty.

He suppressed a sigh and concentrated on the crisis at hand. As he strode, carefully, onto the bridge, he said, "LaFuentes, are we ready?"

"The area's scanned, and I've calibrated the rasers. Hold my beer?"

"By all means, fire away."

They watched the screen as the raser blast left the Impulsive and headed to the NO-BRAINR. It looked like a perfect shot until it veered to the left.

LaFuentes took the miss like a pro. "Recalibrating... firing. Another miss. Trying again. Dammit! Captain, the laws of physics are fluctuating. I get a lock, but the beam misses. Guided torpedo?"

"Beer me."

The torpedo described a crooked and winding path, its programming treating every anomaly as an obstacle to be avoided, yet once it got close to its target, it came to a complete stop, smashed flat, and then exploded.

LaFuentes swore again. "Are there defenses on that thing?"

On the Inconceivable, the captain answered. "Well, sure, but against what we expected to see from an exploding star. That it should use those against a planned attack? That should not have happened."

Suddenly, the Inconceivable's crew started to cheer. "Captain, we're detecting a black hole!"

Vizzini dashed to the nearest science console. He studied the readings, his brows narrowed with concern, then he broke into a smile. "You're right! The physics is different, but it is, in fact, a black hole! Amazing!"

"And you're celebrating?" Much as Jeb liked science, he was not happy to see this experiment suddenly act according to plan. "Vizzini, get out of there."

"Right, right! Helm... Oh, dear."

Jeb pinched the bridge of his nose. "You're still stuck?"

At his own helm, Cruz was pushing buttons, but he, too shook his head, adding, "And the tractor beams still aren't working."

"So also with us," the Rational Plausibility's captain added. "Estimate five minutes before the Inconceivable is irrevocably caught in the gravitational pull of the newly forming black hole—then we're next."

"Time to get creative, people," Jeb said.

A thrill of excitement rippled through the bridge. When the captain gave that command, it not only meant they were in deep doo-doo, but also that the crew had complete license in their efforts to solve the problem. The last time they had had to "get creative," was when the Impulsive had passed through an anomaly that had sent them into the middle of a three-way battle between hostile aliens while en route to a starbase to have the ship fumigated. Someone had picked up a cute, fuzzy pet that turned out to be asexually and prolifically procreative. Even the ship's katt could not keep up with the population. They'd finally solved both problems by teleporting the pests to each of the ships and warping away during the confusion.

Sadly, they had no tribbles to throw at the wonkyverse.

Lt. LaFuentes started by trying to shoot the black hole, under the assumption that if the laws of physics weren't going to work right, it could hardly hurt to try. He was right: it didn't hurt. It didn't help, either.

"Let's replicate a reset button!" one of the second-string bridge crew cried from the bullpen. "If the replicators are really twisting things to alternate purposes, maybe it will reset the universe."

"Or reset us," Smythe replied.

"Do it," Jeb said. "But don't hit it until we're five seconds from death."

The crewman gave her captain a sharp nod and strode into the conference room, which had the nearest replicator. Inside, her heart was beating with joy at being given permission to try her idea as well as with fear that they might actually have to use it.

"Captain," Loreli's voice came over the intercom. "I've been pondering the problem of the replicators, and I think it may apply to our situation. Just like the rules of this universe, the actions of the replicated items correlate to their creators, either species or individual. So if we can find the common link between humans, Commanders Deary and Jardin, and the actions of the NO-BRAINR, perhaps we can undo the damage."

"Then we could send a patch and reprogram the NO-BRAINR to fix what it's done," Smythe suggested, "but we have four minutes to figure out what's wrong."

"The threads!" Doall said. "Inconceivable, look for threads that are off by 90 degrees."

Basil replied by rolling his eyes. "Among all the threads in the altered universe?"

"Right... Um... Bridge to Teleporter room. Dolfrick, we need you to send the Inconceivable Commander Deary's last teleporter record. Hurry—we only have a few minutes. Lieutenant

Cruz, try reversing the polarity of the tractor beam by 90 degrees."

"We already did. No result."

"Try it by forty-five," someone from the bullpen suggested, but everyone scoffed. After all, you can't reverse the polarity by 45 degrees. That's crazy talk.

"Button's done," the crewman declared as she proudly stepped back onto the bridge. "I even gave it a nice clock to count down the time."

She tilted the button for everyone to see. Rather than a digital readout, it was indeed a circular clock face with a minute hand and a second hand. It showed three minutes, five seconds. The clock made faint ticking sounds as it counted down the time to the Inconceivable's doom.

People "ooo"d appreciatively.

Suddenly Smythe snapped his fingers. "Analog! Cruz, reverse the polarity two hundred seventy degrees and try again."

"Aye, sir!" Cruz's hands stabbed at buttons. If he'd had time, he would have replicated a nice dial and installed it. In fact, he made a mental note to suggest it later. There was something satisfying about turning a dial as opposed to punching buttons. However, the results themselves were just as rewarding.

"Got them! Pulling them toward us. It's like dragging a spoon through my nona's chili, but it's moving."

"Your nona made chili?" LaFuentes asked.

"What? You think we ate pasta all the time?"

"Captain," Doall interrupted, "I think that's the key to our 'patch' as well. I've almost got it programmed."

Jeb turned to gape at her. In fact, most of the crew paused in their wild scheming to do the same. This was a new record in Doall-saves-the-day. "What? Just in the time we took to snag the Inconceivable?"

Ellie's cheeks pinked. "Well, the science teams on the Inconceivable and Rational Plausibility are passing me the data, and I'm consolidating it into a program. Is that okay?"

Jeb grinned. "It's good to see you leading a team, Ensign."

From the Security console, Enigo pouted. "So I don't get to shoot the NO-BRAINR after all?"

Doall shrugged apologetically.

From the Inconceivable, Basil said, "No, but you can shoot that star. In fact, every ship should fire all weapons at the star as soon as we reprogram the NO-BRAINR."

"What? Why?" Jeb asked before his chief of security could cheer.

"Because no one wants to give up their warp core, is why! We're going to have to power that star up if it's going to counteract the black hole. Oh, don't ask how. It's a thread thing; you wouldn't understand."

Again, Ellie gave an apologetic shrug. This was beyond her level of math as well, but the Inconceivable science team chimed in agreement it would either work or send them into a mirror universe. She'd never been to a mirror universe. She wondered if her hair was curly there.

"One minute, y'all," the Impulsive warned.

"But I'm pulling the Inconceivable away from the black hole," Cruz protested. "That should have bought us some time."

"Oh, it did," Pulsie replied with electronic amiability, "but that there countdown clock that Ensign Mort made? It's tied itself into my self-destruct sequence."

Ensign Mort squealed and nearly dropped the device. Meanwhile, the Impulsive announced 45 seconds to self-destruct.

"Cancel self-destruct," Jeb cried. "Authorization Jebediah Wisconsin Tiberius, N0-K1ll-I."

"No can do," the Impulsive replied. "It's tied to that damn clock."

"Fix it, bullpen!" Jeb ordered. "Get creative! Doall?"

"Patch is uploading," Doall said. The shiny lines and small objects moving quickly toward the star showed Enigo had begun their barrage without waiting for his command. Good. The other ships were also pounding the star with everything they had.

"Patch complete and accepted. It's rebooting..."

"Fifteen seconds..." Pulsie added.

From the bullpen, the voices of the second string bridge crew were growing frantic as they called out directions and suggestions. The assistant chief engineer rose to assist, but Jeb held up a hand and he sat back down. He had to trust all his crew to solve problems; if the second-stringers weren't up to the task, they would not be on the bridge.

Of course, if Jeb was wrong, in 10 seconds, no one would be.

"Captain, the Inconceivable is moving toward us naturally now," Cruz reported.

Meanwhile, Ensign Mort yanked the hands off the clock and threw them on opposite sides of the bridge.

"Nice out-of-the-box thinking," Pulsie said. "Too bad it didn't work. Five…"

Doall said, "Physics is returning to normal. The black hole is closing,"

"Three…"

"Shoot it!" LaFuentes shouted from his console. Several others were also shouting ideas while Ensign Mort started to quake with panic.

"One."

Ensign Mort shrieked with frustration and slammed her hand on the button.

"Self-destruct de-activated," the Impulsive said. "And to think, just a day ago, I was concerned about scorching on my hull. Kind of puts things into perspective, don't it?"

* * *

Captain's Log, Intergalactic Date 676921.05

One of the frustrating things about being in a time-critical, near-death situation is that I don't have time to get long-winded technical explanations from my crew. It means placing a lot of trust in my crew—who, I'd like to say, have never let me down—but it also means holding back my curiosity until after the crisis.

Once again, the bridge crew met in the conference room for a briefing, while the second-string bridge crew were manning the fort and giving each other high-fives and pats on the back. Loreli had left her quarters and walked trip-free to the bridge. She gave the heroes-of-the-day warm congratulations and thanks before joining the bridge crew. With the Inconceivable and the Rational Plausibility listening on the viewscreens, she explained her insight.

"While Commanders Deary and Jardin were looking for structural reasons for the odd malfunctions of the replicators, I researched all the reported anomalies and found a curious commonality. The toilet paper order, for example, was originally programmed by a Kitenski, who, having traits similar to primitive felines, prefer licking their genitals clean. The turkraken reacted according to human legend. The talking fish, I found in the historical archives; it was apparently a popular and beloved gift in Earth's late twentieth/early twenty-first centuries."

"And the ear drops?" Jeb asked.

"There is a saying among Logics about losing their ears."

Loreli refrained from stating the actual saying, which she'd only learned in the comparative sexuality course she'd taken while the ship was in dry dock. On the view-screen, several of the Rational Plausibility crew shifted their stances. It seemed a casual enough motion, but she knew even this subtle hint of ear-fondling had made them uncomfortable.

She pretended not to notice and continued smoothly, "This led me to conclude that there was at least a species-specific link between the programmers and the unusual actions of the things they replicated, as well as possibly an individual link. Thus, the actions of the NO-

BRAINR resulted not just from the external suggestions of their conversations, but were tied specifically to the unique personalities and experiences of Commanders Deary and Jardin."

Deary nodded. "I see. So, since together, we had discovered how to reverse polarity by 90 degrees, our new device sought to do something similar."

"Right," Doall chimed in. "And since the experiment was happening at a thread level, it made sense that the alterations were, too. Since it wasn't affecting all threads, we looked for threads like those found in you—hence, the teleporter scans. It's a good thing Chief Dour is such a devoted telesubstantialist."

Captain Vizzini clapped his hands together and rubbed them. His gleeful expression was reflected in the faces of all his bridge crew. "We'll be writing papers on this phenomena for years! Speaking on behalf of my crew, we could not be more pleased with the results."

"The experiment was a complete failure," the Logic captain noted.

"I know! Isn't it wonderful?"

The Logic captain allowed himself the luxury of a sigh, a testimony to his deep exasperation with humans in general and those of the Inconceivable in particular.

If Vizzini noticed, he chose to ignore it. "Before we all go our separate ways, we'd like to have the science teams gather on our ship to go over notes—plus, Ensign Doall, naturally. Her insights were most enlightening."

Deary added, "I'd like to go, too, Captain...Captain. Once we're sure physics is completely back to normal, I'd like to shut off the NO-BRAINR and fetch it back to the Impulsive to study it against the second one we created. Perhaps if we can find differences between the two, we might figure out what's going on."

Jeb nodded. "Now that we have normality, that is our top priority. All right, then. You and Ensign Doall take a shuttle and retrieve the device, and then head over to the Inconceivable."

"I look forward to working with you further, Ensign," Fle'ek said.

When the screens went dark, Enigo cooed, "Ooo! Someone's gonna have his ears drop off."

That night, Enigo snuck into Loreli's room using the Jefferies tubes, a time-honored tradition on The Hood. After he squeezed his way out of her vent and had brushed himself off, she made sure to trip and fall into his arms. He told her she was beautiful in pink, and she told him he was brave against main courses. When they kissed, she made sure not to use her tongue.

Later, as they cuddled contentedly on her couch, he blew into her hair and whispered, "I love you."

The next morning, Loreli saw Ellie as she was leaving the teleporter room, stifling a yawn.

"Were you working on the Inconceivable all night?" she asked as she joined in step beside her. They headed to the bridge conference room. Commander Deary had called for a meeting to discuss what they'd found from examination of the NO-BRAINRs.

Ellie's cheeks grew pinker than Loreli's. "Not really. I... Lieutenant Fle'ek invited me back to his ship—but it's not what you think! I mean, yeah, I was with him all night, but it was just our first date. I'm not like that, and we'd only just met and..."

"Relax, Ellie," Loreli said as she slipped an arm through hers. She led her to the nearby restroom, where she produced a brush for Ellie. It was simply to give her an excuse to speak privately, of course. Ellie would never go to a briefing in less than a professional state of attire.

Loreli leaned on a sink in a way that casually invited conversation, a pose she'd learned in ship's sexy training and practiced often. "I'm well versed in art of Logic courtship. There's a reason they say the ears fall off and not some other body part. But may I ask your impression of the evening?"

Ellie's look of relief morphed into one of doubt. She brushed her hair a few times, her gaze turned inward. "Well, at first it was really exciting...but then, it just got long."

They arrived in time to take their seats as the captain entered from the bridge. If anyone had noticed anything unusual between Enigo and Loreli, or about Ellie, they gave no indication, and the trio was glad of it.

Ensign Sisco stood with Commander Deary at one side of the table. As the captain settled into his seat, Deary pulled up an image of the NO-

BRAINR. The image blew apart as he spoke, and then narrowed to one piece and increased magnification.

"We knew something had sabotaged the replicators, but we couldna see how. Even with the scientific equipment on the Inconceivable and knowing approximately what to look for, it took us hours, but we did find it. 'Twas your insight about threads that gave us the key, Ensign."

The magnification had increased, showing them first molecules, then atoms, then strings. Finally, it rested at the thread level. Even with the best viewing technology the Interstellar Union had to offer, the image was grainy and out of focus.

"This is from a programming chip, a line of crystalline logitanium. The thread is known as yarnia, it's one of the most common in the universe. However, if you compare this one to a normal yarnia..."

He pulled up a second image, this one artificially colored yellow. He directed the computer to overlap the two images, then magnify again. There was no dramatic difference between the images, just a subtle variation in length and texture barely apparent. Deary insisted it was not a variation of the equipment, and Ensign Sisco agreed.

Now Sisco spoke. "We checked over a hundred of these threads. Most, but not all, showed anomalies, but not all the same anomaly. We think it's some kind of programming code."

He paused then, waiting for his fellow officers to draw the only rational conclusion. They looked from the diagram to each other, but not even Ellie spoke first. No one wanted to voice the horror of what they'd found.

Finally, the captain spoke. "No wonder we couldn't find prankster or the altered code. No human could have done this. There's only one species with the programming sophistication for this kind of work."

Sisco nodded. "Yes, sir. The Cybers."

Ad Astra—a Space Traipse Movie Review

Captain's Log, Supplemental

Seldom do I have to discipline my crew for getting into fights with each other. When I do, it's usually for an intra-ship competition. Tonight's Movie Night fiasco is a first, however, especially since the fight took place between my Teleporter Chief, Dolfrick Dour, and my Chief of Security, Enigo LaFuentes.

Jeb sat at his desk and stared down the two sullen crewmen. He felt more like a high school principal than a starship captain. "All right then, who started it?"

Just like in high school, the two turned to glare at each other. "He did!"

Jeb sighed. "Uh, huh. Walk me through it. Dolfrick, you chose the movie, correct?"

The Goth teleporter chief nodded. "*Ad Astra*. Yes, sir. It's a science fiction story of the twenty-first century, a subtle masterpiece with valuable lessons concerning the human condition."

Enigo snorted. "The summary said, 'Space pirates,' Captain. I should have known the minute McBride started monologuing about how he felt like an imposter that this was going to be more about some guy's mental issues than an actual science fiction adventure."

Dour looked affronted. "But there are space pirates, Captain. It was a tense moment in the film, and he and his people started laughing."

"Come on! Eight guys in four moon buggies? With guns. But even before that: They were transporting McBride, this big-VIP-type, on a secret mission to save humankind to a secret base on the dark side of the moon...in an open moon buggy. With *two* escorts. Knowing there were so-called space pirates. There's this whole freaking infrastructure on the moon—they had some kind of neon cowboy, for frack's sake!—and they couldn't cobble together some armor, let alone a wikadas shield? I thought it was a comedy!"

"Why wouldn't they shuttle him over?" some morbid curiosity made Jeb ask.

"You'd think because of space pirates, but no!"

Dolfrick sighed. "The lunar pirates were a device to show the chaos of early colonization and territorial rights—a metaphor for the human selfishness that even the grand mission of space colonization was helpless to suppress."

"Oh, a metaphor!" Enigo rolled his eyes. "That explains why they went after a seemingly valueless convoy, wrecked two of the three targets and let the last one get away."

"So this is when the fight started?" Jeb asked, trying to get back to the point.

Dolfrick shook his head. "No, Captain. I was willing to suffer in patient silence."

Enigo nodded sagely. "Is that like a metaphor for the movie?"

The Goth teleporter chief curled his lip. "No, but I did identify even more poignantly when McBride spoke with such eloquence about suppressing his rage."

Enigo pursed his lips wisely and steepled his fingers. Apparently, he'd decided to play the straight man. "Ah, yes. The rage of the Space Baboons."

Jeb blinked. "Baboons?"

"In space, sir," Enigo said.

"What were the baboons doing in space?"

"Raging, sir," Enigo deadpanned.

Dolfrick closed his eyes as if calling upon a higher power for patience and answered. "They were the victims of biomedical experimentation that escaped and killed the crew aboard the space station. McBride's ship to Mars answered their mayday."

"Which made no mention of violent primates."

"There wasn't time!" Dolfrick snapped.

"What? No time to say, 'Mayday! Mayday! Marauding murderous monkeys'? That was just the first mistake, Captain. The captain of McBride's ship puts a top-secret mission in jeopardy to answer a cryptic mayday. McBride doesn't pull rank to stop him—and don't give me the 'then you have to tell us your mission' BS. Then, out of spite, they send the *VIP*—the whole reason for this trip—into an unknown situation and potentially dangerous environment. They split the party..."

Dolfrick interrupted. "Needless to say, the lieutenant used this tense, exciting scene as a training exercise."

"Tense? McBride stopped in the middle of a retreat to try to duct tape the faceplate of a dead man. Duct tape, Captain. The whole faceplate. To take the dead captain back to the other ship— through the vacuum of space. Then he waxed poetic about how he identified with the rage of the space baboon."

Jeb rubbed his chin. "You laughed again?"

Dolfrick answered, "And made monkey sounds."

"And that's when the fight started?"

"No, sir, it was when he started shouting about the Dread Oog."

Enigo sighed. "Sir, you have to understand. There was this big mystery about whether or not Neptune had been invaded by extra-terrestrial life. With everyone acting so stupidly and the constant self-affirming psych evals that accomplished *nada*, I was sure the human race was under some kind of mind control. So when I saw the reprogramming chambers—"

"They were comfort rooms!" Dolfrick said, his ire breaking past his usual sullen smolder to edge toward space baboon rage. "McBride was in a comfort room. He was confronting his fears concerning the rejection by his father. And in this touching scene, the lieutenant starts yelling, 'Fight the Oog!'"

Enigo said, "I'm telling you, sir: Those were Dread Oog torture chambers, just like from the Occupation Years on the Hood."

"They were Martian comfort rooms. They had a comfortable chair where you sit and meditate while surrounded by comforting images of Earth."

"Comforting? He was surrounded by flocks of huge, shadowy birds. Six-foot birds, Captain. They were everywhere. And the ocean crashing in on all sides? How is that comforting?"

Dolfrick grimaced, seeing his point, but pressed on. "There were flowers."

"The flowers were taller than me."

"They were colorful and beautiful."

"The chrysanthemums were breathing!"

At last Jeb saw from the expression on the men's faces the answer he was looking for. He said to Dour, "And that's when you hit the lieutenant?"

Enigo answered cheerily. "He didn't just hit me, sir. He bounded over two rows of seats and fended off my minions to get to me. It was fracking beautiful, sir. Real space baboon rage." He turned to Dolfrick, "Seriously, dude. I didn't think you had it in you."

Jeb rubbed his brows, in part to show his frustration, but also to hide the grin that threatened to show on his face. "All right. For the next two weeks, you are both confined to quarters when not on duty. Lieutenant LaFuentes, you will brush up on movie etiquette. There's an old Earth saying: There's a special place in Hell for people who talk in theaters.

"Chief Dour, I suggest the next time you pick a movie, you be more careful about how you represent it. Dismissed."

The two stood, saluted smartly, and left the room. They said nothing as they entered the lazivator together. Once the doors closed, Enigo said, "So, if it wasn't the Dread Oog, who were the aliens doing the mind control?"

Dolfrick sighed as deeply and painfully as McBride might have on his decades-long trip to Neptune. "There was no mind control. There were no aliens. McBride's father fails to find evidence of extraterrestrial life and kills himself. McBride, meanwhile, comes to terms with the ennui of our race's isolation."

Enigo shook his head. "You're sure it's not a comedy?"

"Only when you watch it."

The fun continues!

Ready for Book 3? Click to get it on Amazon.

Thanks for Reading!

I can't believe it's been three years since I started writing the Space Traipse stories. I started these when I was in a stressful place in my life. They were a low-pressure way to keep writing and have some fun. I knew that life would get better—and it has!—but I did not expect that I would fall in love with these characters or that other people would love the stories so. Thank you, all of you who read the blog, follow Space Traipse on Facebook, and ask about the next story collection. You can find the past and current stories here with their links: https://karinafabian.com/books/space-traipse/.

I'd like to thank the beta readers who so generously gave their time to seek out my typos: Tamara Wilhite, John Earle, Paul McDermott, Deborah Cullins Smith, Jane Lebak (and her kids), Kerrie Lapoehn (hey, cuz!), and Steve Lumbert (my dear dad!). It's so nice to have great friends who are also great writers and readers. Thanks, guys—I hope you enjoyed the book.

I no longer dream of being a best seller, but I still enjoy knowing that my stories are read. Many thanks to those who reviewed Space Traipse on Amazon and have told their friends. Please do so again with this one—reviews help.

I have an intermittent newsletter, so if you want to know about my latest works and news, please subscribe: https://tinyurl.com/fabianspacenews.

Thanks again for joining me in my fun.

About the Author

Karina Fabian lives on Ground Zero for potential Xindi attack, but doesn't mind, since she can watch rocket launches from her backyard. In 1990, she married a steely-eyed spaceman, Rob, who is now the President of Rocket Crafters. She writes fictional space travel while he works to make it true. In the meantime, they raised four great kids.

Keep in Touch

If you want to learn about future books, please

- Sign up for my newsletter. https://fabianspace.substack.com/subscribe for more stories, updates and a free book!
- Visit my website (https://karinafabian.com)
- Follow me on Facebook: https://www.facebook.com/Karina-Fabian-Speculative-Fiction-with-a-Grin-2233839790277963
- Join HuFleet—follow the Impulsive on Facebook: https://www.facebook.com/sthmb/

There's More Fun in FabianSpace!

Thank you for buying this book. If you enjoyed it, click to see the others in this series or discover one of the other worlds of FabianSpace.

Science Fiction

Space Traipse: Hold My Beer: Redneck ingenuity and common sense in a Star Trek-ish universe. Enjoy the adventures of the HMB Impulsive.

The Rescue Sisters: Intrepid women doing dangerous missions in space for the love of God and humankind.

The Old Man and the Void: Dex is a relic hunter on the edge of the black hole, desperate for the catch of a lifetime.

Jovian Heat: As the next Great Storm of Jupiter rises, Cass must find the father of a baby in peril—but the father died before the child was conceived.

Fantasy

DragonEye: Vern's a snarky dragon on the wrong side of the Interdimensional Gap, solving crimes, battling evil, and saving the universes on an all-too-regular basis.

Madness of Kanaan: Deryl isn't crazy; he's psychic, and aliens of two worlds thinks he can save them. Maybe he can—but can he regain his sanity in the process?

Horror

Neeta Lyffe, Zombie Exterminator: Neeta's an average exterminator, taking out bugs, rodents, and the undead. Can she keep her friends alive, pay her bills, and find romance?

Frightliner and Other Tales of the Supernatural (with Colleen Drippé): Truck-driving vampires terrorizing the road, Southern women doing what needs doing, a zombie wedding—a great story collection for horror lovers.